ZEBRA STORM

Elizabeth Laird was born in New Zealand but when she was two the family moved to England. Since then she has travelled to the furthest corners of the world and has encountered all kinds of animals. On one adventure she became lost at night in a Kenyan game reserve, coming a little too close to an angry rhino and narrowly avoiding buffalo and elephants. Her experience of the wild animals of Africa has helped her write the *Wild Things* series.

She is the award-winning author of *Red Sky in the Morning*, *Kiss the Dust*, *Secret Friends* (shortlisted for the 1997 Carnegie Medal) and many other children's novels.

Elizabeth Laird has been helped in her research for *Wild Things* by wildlife experts and local people in Kenya, whose lives are constantly touched by the animals amongst which they live.

WILD THINGS

ZEBRA STORM

Elizabeth Laird

MACMILLAN CHILDREN'S BOOKS

Series consultant: Dr Shirley Strum
with the support of Dr David Western,
past director of the Kenya Wildlife Service

First published 1999 by Macmillan Children's Books
a division of Macmillan Publishers Limited
25 Eccleston Place, London SW1W 9NF
Basingstoke and Oxford
www.macmillan.co.uk

Associated companies throughout the world

ISBN 0 330 37153 3

1 3 5 7 9 8 6 4 2

A CIP catalogue record for this book is available from
the British Library.

Phototypeset by Intype London Ltd
Printed and bound in Great Britain by Mackays of Chatham plc, Kent

For Kinyaga Ole Nderepa, James Ole Kinyage, and the many Maasai Warriors, who welcomed me to their lodge, took me to their village, sang me their songs and talked to me about the rare and beautiful animals amongst which they live.

The zebra stallion's black hooves stirred up flurries of dust from the earth, which had been baked to an iron hardness by searing months of drought. A gust of wind picked the dust up, and blew it in pale brown streams across the dried-up bed of the water hole.

The zebra stallion lowered his great head and walked across the bare ground, where cool water used to lap the reeds. Now the dried earth was cracked with deep fissures, and pitted with a hundred animal tracks, left here when the mud was still soft enough to take the imprint of paws and hooves, birds' claws and elephants' feet. Yesterday, a few muddy puddles had still remained, enough to partially slake the zebra's thirst, but today, even those had gone.

He lifted his head. He would have to leave his territory, which he had guarded as his own for half a lifetime, and make the dangerous, half-remembered journey to the river. He would have to find his way round barbed wire fences, and cross roads where death might race at him out of nowhere at unimaginable speeds. He would be lucky to reach the river alive.

But he knew of nowhere else where water could be found. He tossed his head, sending ripples down his stiff crest-like mane, and set off. He travelled all day, and when evening came, the smell of the river was in his nostrils. He snorted through his soft nostrils, and broke into a trot.

In his excitement, he didn't notice the shadowy figure of a man, who, himself half-starved with hunger, was stalking him through the brittle dead grass.

Ironically, it was a snake that saved the zebra's life. It shot up out of the grass, hissing and waving its head, ready for a strike. The zebra reared at the precise moment that the raised spear left the man's hand. It had been aimed with deadly accuracy at the zebra's heart, but instead plunged into his rump, making a deep wound that marked the perfect black and white of his stripes with an ugly gash of red.

The zebra, stung with fear and pain, turned and bolted away from the river. He was going south now, running blindly into a region he had never entered before. He halted at last, trembling with pain and exhaustion. He listened, but there was no sound of a chase.

Night had fallen. Weak with thirst and loss of blood, he was almost ready to give up, to lie down and wait for whatever predator would come upon *him. But then to his keen nostrils came the smell he longed for. Water wasn't far away.*

He turned and began to walk, his head drooping, through the dry scrub towards a cleft in a distant rocky ridge.

The moon, rising an hour later, caught the silvery cascade of drops that fell from his muzzle as he lifted his head from a clear cool stream.

1

A LETTER FROM NANYUKI

Joseph stood at the side of the busy main road which ran through the Kenyan town of Nanyuki and looked across at the big glass-fronted garage and car showroom on the other side. Trucks, cars and matatu buses crammed with people raced along the road, hooting their horns impatiently as they careered past a camel driver with his train of soft-footed camels.

Joseph bit a fingernail nervously. This was the place. He knew it was.

He put his hand in his pocket and pulled out a crumpled letter. It was written in careful English and addressed to Sarah, Joseph's mother. It was signed Reverend Samuel Ndungu and it contained the first news of Joseph's father that his mother had received for the past seven years.

Dear Mrs Sarah, the letter said. *I think it is a long time that you have not heard my name. You can remember me? I am the friend of Kioko, your husband, who went to Zimbabwe seven years ago with me and some other persons to look for work. We separated from*

*each other after some time and I became a
Pastor in my church. I am writing now because
I have some news of your husband Kioko. He
is working in the big garage in Nanyuki, where
new cars are available to sell.*

*I know your husband well. His heart is
proud. His desire is to return to his family with
great riches. But riches have not come to him.
I think he will not return to you because of
some feeling of shame.*

*Mrs Sarah, Kioko needs his family, and his
love for you all is great. He has left you for
seven years. It is wrong of him. It is too long
for a lady to be alone, but perhaps you can
forgive him. You and Kioko have a son, your
boy, Joseph. The boy needs his father.*

*Mrs Sarah, Nanyuki is far from Nairobi, but
it will be very good if you send Kioko a
message, or send your son to find him there.*

*By the Grace of God,
Rev Samuel Ndungu*

Memories of his father churned round in
Joseph's mind. He had been five or six years old
when Kioko Mutua had left home, but he could
remember only stern frowning eyes, a harsh voice
raised in anger, and painful blows on his back
and head. He couldn't recall a single loving
embrace or kind word. His father had terrified
him. He'd been glad when he'd gone away.

It was so unfair, thought Joseph. For weeks he'd been looking forward to this expedition to Mountview Ranch with his friends, Afra and Tom, and Prof, Afra's father. Mountview Ranch was a special place, a beautiful wildlife reserve in the north of Kenya, where rhinos still lived, and the rare Grevy zebra roamed across the huge spreading grasslands. He'd been looking forward to it, anyway, until Sarah, his mother, had spoiled it all.

'You will be passing through Nanyuki,' Sarah had said. 'I have asked Prof and he says you will stop there for your lunch. You can go to the garage and look for your father. The Reverend Samuel is right, Joseph. It is our duty to find him.'

But I don't want to, thought Joseph. I really, really, don't want to.

A ragged child appeared suddenly beside Joseph. He was holding a little carved zebra, the black stripes painted crookedly on the carved wood.

'*Rahisi sana*,' he said in Swahili. 'Very cheap. Only ten shillings. You buy?'

'*Hapana*, no,' said Joseph, pushing him gently aside.

Voices from the café behind him made him turn his head. Tom, Afra and Prof were finishing their lunch. He'd only slipped out for a minute, saying he wanted to buy something in one of the shops

6

further down the road. He hadn't told them about the letter, or about his father.

Prof would want to get going any minute now, to finish the journey to Mountview Ranch before it got dark. If he didn't get back to the café soon they'd come out and look for him.

It was now or never.

He dived across the road without looking, almost into the path of a heavy lorry. The driver sounded his horn, leaned out of his window and shouted furiously.

Joseph took no notice. He was already dashing on long legs up to the imposing double doors of the car showroom. He stepped inside.

It was a big bright space, filled with shiny new cars and overbearingly large agricultural machines. Light glanced off the polished glass and metal. A couple of *mzungu** farmers were inspecting a huge yellow tractor, talking loudly in confident voices.

Joseph stood inside the door, trying to pluck up the courage to walk across the daunting open space to the desk at the far end, where a man in a smart blue jacket was talking in rapid Swahili on the telephone.

The man finished his conversation and put the receiver down. Then he looked up and saw Joseph. He frowned.

* white people

7

'Who are you?' he called out in a peremptory voice. 'What do you want?'

His words echoed round the showroom.

The *mzungus* turned to look at Joseph. He felt the blood surge up into his face. Quickly, he walked up to the desk. He didn't want the embarrassment of being shouted at again.

'Excuse me, sir,' he said. 'I'm looking for – for my . . . '

His voice trailed away. The man was looking him up and down, his scornful eyes taking in Joseph's casual trainers and T-shirt.

This is not the place, his hard eyes seemed to be saying, for scruffy boys like you.

Joseph began to feel irritated. This man was a salesman, not some big chief.

'I'm looking for Kioko Mutua,' he said more bravely. 'I . . . he works here.'

The man jerked his head towards a small door at the back of the showroom.

'If you wish to see one of the mechanics, go straight round to the yard,' he said. 'Only our customers are allowed in here.'

Joseph frowned sharply, offended by the man's tone, but then the full meaning of what he'd said sank in, and his stomach gave a kick.

He knows his name, he thought. He's here! He must be one of the mechanics!

His legs felt oddly heavy as he pushed open the door that led out of the showroom and down some steps into the big yard of the garage. The sun was beating right onto his face and he had to screw up his eyes to see.

Cars and agricultural machinery were parked in a series of sheds round the sides of the yard. At first, to his relief, he had thought the place was deserted, but then he heard the rattle of tools and a murmur of voices, and looking to the left he saw two men in dark blue overalls, who were working together on a car's engine under its opened bonnet.

It's him! He's one of them, he thought wildly. He couldn't move. He stared with fearful fascination at the blue-clad back nearest to him, watching the man's powerful shoulders move about as he worked on the engine. His stomach was rising with the old familiar sick fear his father had always inspired in him. He felt five years old again.

No, a voice was saying inside his head. I don't want to do this. I don't have to do this. No. No.

He was about to turn and tiptoe back into the showroom, braving the salesman's anger, when one of the men looked up and saw him. He nudged the other man, who straightened up too. With a little gasp of relief, Joseph saw that they were young, much younger than his father would be. The nearest one was wiping his sleeve across his forehead where beads of sweat glittered on his dark skin.

'You are looking for someone?' he called out in a friendly voice.

'No,' said Joseph. 'It's OK. I . . . I lost my way. I'm going now.'

The second man was staring at him intently.

'Have you been here before?' he said. 'I know you, don't I?'

The first man laughed.

'You see his face every day,' he said. 'Look at him. He is exactly like Kioko Mutua.'

He came up to Joseph and looked down disbelievingly into Joseph's face.

'It's amazing! You are like Kioko Mutua exactly! Are you his relative? Did you come here to visit him?'

'I'm his son,' said Joseph, responding unwillingly to the man's friendliness.

'His son!' The man shook his head. 'He is a very secret person, Kioko Mutua. He never told us he had a son.'

Joseph's lips tightened with anger. His father's friends didn't even know that he had a son at all!

The man was still talking.

'That Kioko, he is always alone, too much alone. He never speaks of anything about himself. Anyway, you are not lucky today. Kioko is out of town. He is delivering a truck to a ranch up country.'

Joseph felt an odd mixture of relief and anticlimax. He started to back away. 'Thank you for telling me. Excuse me for disturbing you.'

The man laughed.

'You are not disturbing us. We are very interested to see the son of Kioko Mutua. Where are you living?'

'In Nairobi.'

'Nairobi?' The man looked concerned. 'And you have come so far, this long way to Nanyuki, to find your father? Are you staying here? In which place? I will tell Kioko so that he can find you. He is returning today, I think.'

'I'm not staying in Nanyuki,' said Joseph, taking another step backwards. 'We're only passing through. I'm with friends. We're on holiday. We're going on, up north.'

'Where? Where will you be staying?' the man persisted. 'Who is taking you?'

'We'll be at Mountview Ranch,' said Joseph unwillingly. He was reluctant to give anything away, but he didn't want to seem rude. 'And I'm with Professor Tovey and his daughter. But tell him – my father – that it doesn't matter. We'll only be there for a few days. Tell him it's not important. Really, it doesn't matter.'

Then he turned and ran to the big double gates at the far end of the yard, not stopping to take a breath until he was through them.

Afra and Tom were already outside the café when he got back, waiting for Prof to pay the bill.

Tom was examining one of the wooden zebras the same ragged little boy was showing him.

'My brother would like one of these,' he said.

'Little Jimmy?' said Afra. 'That's so dumb, Tom. He'd think it was a candy and go "Goo goo", and lick it all over, and the paint would come off and poison his little insides.'

'Well I want one anyway,' said Tom. 'I think they're great.'

The little boy, sensing victory, thrust the zebra even closer to Tom's face.

'Very cheap,' he kept saying anxiously. 'Very good. Only twenty shillings.'

'Twenty shillings?' Joseph said incredulously in Swahili. 'Are you crazy? You said ten shillings to me.'

The boy looked at him pleadingly.

'They're *mzungus*,' he said, reverting to Swahili too. 'They can pay. Don't spoil my sale, brother.'

'They're my friends!' said Joseph indignantly. 'You're cheating them!'

The little boy stared contemptuously at him for a moment, then saw another car pull up outside the café. He ran up to it, waving his carved zebra.

'Only 25 shillings!' he cried. 'Look, very nice! Very fine zebra!'

'Oh, he's gone,' said Tom, disappointed.

Prof appeared.

'Come on, you guys. Let's go. Finished your shopping, Joseph?'

Joseph nodded. He felt bad. Why had he interfered? Now no one was happy. Tom hadn't got his zebra and the little boy hadn't earned himself some much needed money.

What sort of holiday is this going to be? he thought bitterly, climbing into the hot Land Rover beside Afra.

2

THE BAO GAME

Joseph picked up a handful of smooth round pebbles and dropped them three by three into the egg-cup shaped hollows in the rocks. There were two parallel rows of eleven holes, forming an open air *bao* game-board. It was cut into a flat rock that shelved out of the hillside above the vast plain of Mountview Ranch.

'You have to finish up without any stones on your side, and you have to try to get rid of mine,' he said to Tom. 'You do it like this.'

Tom watched closely, then started dropping his own pebbles into the holes. For a moment, the only sound was the rattle of pebbles, Afra's rasping breath as she watched, and the distant crunching noise made by Prof's feet, as he wandered round the hillside below.

Joseph grunted with satisfaction and raised his head.

'I've won. Look, none of my pebbles are left.'

Tom frowned down at the game.

'You went so fast I couldn't see what you were doing. Let's play again.'

'Hey, it's my turn.' Afra was already picking up Joseph's pebbles and laying them out again.

Joseph stood up and stretched. He wasn't in the mood for playing games anyway. He moved away from the others and sat down at the side of the warm smooth rock, letting his legs dangle over the edge.

He rested his chin on his hands and looked out over the grassland, which swept away, uninterrupted, to the distant blue Nyambeni Mountains. Their crests were dark against the pale blue sky, but the early mist still clouded their lower slopes so that they seemed to float above the horizon.

It was early and the sun was still low. It cast a warm rich light on the outcrop of rock, making it glow as golden as honey. Below it, the bare dry ground was peppered with rough fragments of sparkling pink and white quartz.

Over the past few months, drought had held the land in a ferocious grip. The wispy grass was brittle and yellowed and the few scattered acacia trees looked dry and grey-brown under a coating of dust. Only the line of fever trees by the stream below looked alive. Their leaves shone out as shiny and green as emeralds.

Behind him Joseph could hear Afra crowing with delight as she made a clever move, and Tom's answering grunt of disgust. A blacksmith's plover called out its high rising song, and weaver birds chirruped round their nests in the acacia tree below. There were no other sounds. The quietness was soothing.

Yesterday's encounter at the garage in Nanyuki had left Joseph jangled and sore. The same refrain had been going round and round in his head ever since he'd run out of the garage yard.

He's been living only a few hours away from us all these years and he never even bothered to let Mama know he was alive. He's mean. Really mean. It's a bad thing to say but I'm going to say it. I hate my own father.

A shout from Afra made him turn his head.

'Look! Zebras!'

Tom, whose hand was hovering indecisively over the carved holes, his forehead wrinkled with concentration, hardly bothered to look up.

'So? Those aren't the rare zebras. They're the ordinary ones, and we saw millions of them yesterday. At least a hundred, anyway.'

'No, but look, will you?' Afra said impatiently. 'They're giving themselves a dust bath. Oh, aren't they just amazing?'

Joseph screwed his eyes up to see against the sun. A herd of ten or more zebras was crossing the plain below. They paused one after the other, as if they were queuing, at a patch of bare ground and took turns to roll in the dust, their fat bellies barrelling from side to side, making the dust rise in pale clouds. As one trotted on, the next one took his place, stopping first to sniff the ground, then letting his knees buckle beneath him as he went into his roll.

The last one, coming out of the dust, seemed to get his legs tangled, and he looked so comical as he staggered to his feet that everyone burst out laughing and even Joseph smiled.

'They're bachelors,' said Prof's voice behind him. 'They live in their own little herds away from the females.'

'Like male elephants do,' said Tom, who had forgotten the pebble game and was watching the zebras with fascination. He caught Joseph's eye and they both nodded, remembering the young male elephant they'd encountered once in the forests on Mount Kenya.

The zebras were walking away into the distance, and were soon no more than a faint blur against the dusty brown earth. Prof sat down on a rock beside Joseph. Sweat glistened on his freckled face and his breath was uneven.

'Where have you been, Prof?' asked Joseph. 'You look tired.'

'I was scrambling round on the flat area behind this hill,' said Prof, 'looking for these.'

He put a roughly hewn pointed stone the size of a man's hand down on the rock beside Joseph. Joseph looked at it curiously.

'What is it?' he asked.

'It's an axe,' said Prof. 'Made by our ancestors about 30,000 years ago.'

Joseph picked it up and held it. It fitted comfortably into his hand. He could see the marks where its maker had hit it with another stone to chip pieces off and shape it into a tool.

'30,000? You mean there were people here 30,000 years ago? People like us?'

'Pretty much like us. They didn't have too much in the way of technology, of course, but they weren't exactly dumb. On the contrary. You try making a stone axe like this. You have to judge it just right, get the chips right where you want them to go. These guys were super skilled crafts people.'

'That's it! I beat you!'

Afra's delighted crow made Prof turn his head.

'What are you kids doing? Oh, I see you found the old *bao* game.'

'Old?' said Tom. 'You mean you knew it was here?'

'Sure I did.' Prof leaned over and felt the smooth round holes with his long fingers. 'I checked it out when I came to Mountview Ranch the first time to do the original archaeological survey. It's a nice example. About 5,000 years old, I guess.'

Tom reared back from the rows of stones in awe, as if he was afraid he might damage them.

'Wow! You mean they're ancient? You mean people have been playing this game all that time? It's—'

He stopped, lost for words.

'Grandfather taught me to play this game,' said Joseph, 'and his grandfather taught him, and his grandfather taught him, I suppose, and it goes back like that for 5,000 years.'

'Longer than that,' said Prof. 'There are much older examples than this one.'

Joseph stretched out his arm and ran a finger round one of the smooth weathered holes. He felt a shiver of awe. Everyone sat in silence for a moment.

'It's not surprising,' said Tom at last, pulling the peak of his cap down over his thick blond thatch of hair to keep the sun off his reddening nose, 'that humans beat all the other animals and became the rulers of the world. We're so clever and quick and brainy. And we're busy all the time. I mean, look down there, at those gazelles, and those waterbuck by the stream. They just eat and sort of mess about all day. They don't make things or build houses or invent cars or anything.'

'So you think that's not clever?' said Afra. 'We've messed up the planet enough all on our own, using up the water and cutting down the trees and polluting everything and stuff like that. Anyway, we're not that brilliant. We have a crummy sense of smell, and our eyes aren't that great either.'

'Who says?' said Tom, waggling his head at

Afra and batting his eyelids up and down very fast. 'You might be as blind as a bat, but my eyes are great, thank you very much.'

Joseph smiled half-heartedly.

'Tom, when you do that, you look like a baboon.'

'A baboon?' Tom screwed up his eyes trying to remember exactly what a baboon did, then he began smacking his lips up and down over his teeth.

'Like this, you mean?'

Afra laughed. She loved baboons. She began to make chattering noises, and took hold of Tom's arm, pretending to groom it like a baboon would.

Joseph snorted.

'You don't look like baboons at all. More like crazy humans!'

Afra suddenly remembered the beginning of the argument.

'Well anyway,' she said, dropping Tom's arm, 'I bet those gazelles down there can see a million times better than you. I bet they can spot a lion a mile away. And you haven't even noticed the snake right there beside your foot.'

Tom looked down. Something long and sinuous lay on the shelf of rock below. It was almost touching his shoe.

'Aarghh!' he shrieked, leaping to his feet.

'Only joking,' said Afra. 'It's only the root of a tree.'

Tom glared at her. If she'd been Joseph he'd have caught her in a headlock, and they'd have staggered around for a bit and had a good old wrestling match, but he didn't fight with girls.

'Sorry,' said Afra, stifling a giggle. 'I couldn't resist.'

Her laughter was usually infectious, but Joseph didn't even smile. He wasn't in the mood for teasing and playing around today.

It's not fair, he thought bitterly. I was looking forward so much to coming here. And now that letter has spoiled everything.

Behind him, he was aware of Tom, squatting on the rock, muttering under his breath. He was staring intently out across the parched landscape, anxious to see something that would prove the excellence of his eyesight.

'Look there! Warthogs!' he said at last, triumphantly.

The warthogs were hard to spot as they ran through the yellow grass. Only their tails, sticking straight up into the air, gave them away. As they came nearer, Joseph could see their comical reddish manes flopping over their shoulders.

'There's another animal,' said Prof, pointing to a dark figure who was striding down towards the stream below. 'Homo Sapiens Africanus.'

'That's not an animal,' said Tom. He hadn't quite recovered from his fright and his voice sounded indignant. 'It's a person.'

'Humans are animals,' said Prof peaceably. 'We're a species of primate. Very sophisticated animals, but animals all the same.'

'Isn't it weird,' said Afra, 'how tourists come to Africa from Europe and America and Japan and everywhere and they only want to look at animals? I mean, non-human animals. They don't bother to meet Africans or talk to them at all.'

The man had reached the stream now. He wore only a scarlet *shuka* over one shoulder, leaving his legs and his other shoulder bare. He walked with a long easy stride, covering the ground fast but with no apparent hurry. Even from this distance the watchers on the hillside could see that he carried a spear.

Joseph, watching him, felt confused. He and his schoolfriends in Nairobi usually laughed at country tribal people, with their superstitions and their funny little huts and their weird clothes and coloured beads. But he didn't want Tom and Afra and Prof, who were *mzungus* after all, to laugh at this fellow Kenyan too. Anyway, there was something about the way the man walked, a kind of lordliness, a sort of superior grace, that impressed him.

'African people are not interesting to tourists,' he said at last, knowing that he sounded defensive but unable to stop himself. 'They do not wish to understand our culture.'

Afra shot him a mischievous look.

'I bet you don't know anything about the culture of that guy down there. He's not a townie like you.'

Joseph rose to the bait.

'You're more of a townie than I am,' he said. 'Anyway, you call yourself half-Ethiopian and you cannot even say ten words in their language.'

Afra's brows snapped together.

'Why are you so cranky today? What's got into you, anyway?'

He saw that he'd hurt her.

'Nothing,' he mumbled. 'Sorry.'

Tom was looking from one to the other.

'I don't get it,' he said. 'What do you mean, Joseph doesn't know about that guy's culture? They're both Africans, aren't they?'

Joseph shook his head.

'Being African, that is not so important. You are European, but not all Europeans are the same. I mean, do you know all about Russians, or Italians, or – or people from Sweden? That man, his tribe is different from my tribe. He speaks another language, eats different food, has so many customs and dances and songs and ideas that are different from mine.'

'What tribe is he, then?' said Tom curiously. 'Isn't he Kamba, like you?'

'No. He is Maasai,' said Joseph. 'He is a warrior.'

'Oh boy, am I glad I'm not a Maasai warrior,'

said Afra, rolling her eyes towards the man. He had been following a track along the valley floor and was now disappearing round the side of the hill. 'They have to go through all kinds of initiation stuff and sleep out in the open and fight battles. Oh, and they don't eat anything except meat, and when they haven't got meat they don't eat anything at all. They just drink milk mixed with cow's blood.'

'What?' said Tom, appalled. 'They drink blood?'

'Sure they do. They take a bit from the cows' necks. They say it doesn't hurt the cow, but I guess it must, a bit.'

'The Maasai really love their cows,' said Joseph. The horror in Tom's face was making him feel prickly. 'They look after them and give them names and dream about them as if they were their own children.'

'No, but I mean not eating anything except for meat and drinking blood,' said Tom, who was really shocked. 'It must be awful. I'd just throw up. And what about bread, and chips, and fruit and chocolate and . . . and biscuits and stuff? How could you live without any of that?'

'You can if you have to,' Joseph said huffily. 'Most of those things are not good for your health, anyway.'

'My mum always makes me eat healthy stuff,' said Tom, grimacing. 'She tries to, anyway.'

'Sarah's practically given up on me,' said Afra.

'Yes,' said Tom. 'But she's not a real mum. She's only a housekeeper.'

'Only a housekeeper?'

Joseph and Afra spoke together, turning angry faces towards Tom.

'She is a real mother,' said Joseph. 'She's my mother.'

'And she's practically my mom too, thank you very much,' said Afra. 'She brought me up.'

'OK, OK,' said Tom. 'Sorry I spoke.'

Prof had been exploring further along the rock. He had found another set of holes, so badly weathered by the wind and rain that they were practically invisible.

'Those old ancestors of yours again, Joseph,' he said. 'Looks like they had a real old tournament going here.'

The word 'ancestors' brought Joseph's mind wheeling straight back to the thought of his father again.

What if those men at the garage tell him about me? he thought. What will he think? I told them I was staying here. If he cared about me at all, he'd come here and look for me. But he won't come. I know he won't. And if he does, I don't care. I won't bother talking to him. Then he'll know.

The others had stood up and were beginning to make their way back up the hill towards the Land Rover. Slowly, Joseph followed them.

3

MOUNTVIEW RANCH

It was a long drive back across the rolling hills and plains of Mountview to the lodge house at the far end of the ranch. The sun was high in the sky now, and the last wisps of early morning mist, that had nestled in the distant valleys and circled round the far peaks of Mount Kenya, were drifting away. The freshness of early morning had gone, and the baked earth looked dry and dusty again.

'Prof, stop! Look, there's a herd of elephants by the stream!' Afra called out suddenly. Prof drew up, and for a while they paused to watch the elephants grazing, lifting their trunks as if in slow motion to crop leaves from the trees, or to scoop up long switches of the grass that still grew lushly down by the water.

Joseph leaned out of the back window. A group of giraffes were grazing almost in front of him, their sides the colour of cinnamon gingerbread. They bent their long necks down gracefully to nibble the sparse shoots of the low growing whistling thorn. Beyond them, the unfenced land swept down to the stream, then undulated gently up to a ridge beyond which Mount Kenya's jagged summit rose against the sky. Dotted about on the vast landscape were Thomson's gazelle, a whole herd of impala and a few single eland, their heavy heads raised to stare curiously at the stationary vehicle and its quiet human occupants.

Joseph felt a stab of regret.

I don't know anything about animals, he thought sadly. Not like Grandfather. He knows them from the inside. When he was a kid people just lived in the middle of them and he must have walked among animals every day. It's so different, living in a city.

His thoughts jerked on, coming round again, inevitably, to the same theme.

Whose fault is it, anyway, if I'm a townic? It's his! It's all his! If he hadn't left us, Mama wouldn't have had to go on working so hard. We could have spent more time in the village with Grandfather and he would have taught me things.

Prof put the Land Rover into gear and drove on.

'We'll have to move a bit faster than this,' he said. 'I've got work to do today.'

'Oh stop, Prof, please stop!' Afra breathed. 'Look, there!'

Everyone turned their heads to see what she was pointing at. Two ostriches were running alongside the Land Rover. The one in front was a female, her drab brown feathers hardly standing out against the dusty land behind her. But the male, who loped hungrily after her, was a magnificent creature, his back feathers black, his pinions a rich creamy white. He was trying to attract the female's attention, but she seemed to take no notice of him and trotted coolly on. The male stopped and began a kind of dance. He subsided to the ground in a rustle of feathers, and began to wave his white pinions, rolling his body from side to side as he did so in a rocking rhythm while he laid his long neck down along his back, writhing his head to and fro.

She doesn't want you, Joseph thought sourly. What are you making all that fuss about? She can manage quite well alone. Why don't you just give up and go away?

A sudden voice behind him made him jump. He turned his head. Two men, their sandalled feet silent in the soft dust of the track, had come up unheard behind the Land Rover. They were middle-aged, and the scarlet *shukas* that hung from their shoulders were a little frayed around the edge. Their earlobes had been pierced with such large holes that they stretched almost down to their shoulders.

'*Sopa*,' they said, smiling at Prof.

'That means "hello" in Maa,' said Joseph under his breath to Afra. He'd learned the word once from his uncle, Titus.

'What's Maa?'

'The Maasai language.'

'Wow.' She looked impressed. 'How did you know that?'

'I just did,' he said.

'Not bad for a townie,' she said, grinning at him.

Joseph saw that she wanted to make friends again and his spirits lifted a little.

Prof was leaning out of the window, pumping the two men's hands with enthusiastic shakes.

'*Ol murrani*, Peter! *Sopa* Lomunyak,' he was saying. 'It's great to see you. Why are you here?'

'We heard you were coming to this place,' Peter, the younger man, said in his singsong Maasai accent. 'We have come to visit you.'

'We're on our way back to our lodge,' said Prof, leaning out of his window even further to open the back door of the Land Rover. 'Come with us. We can talk there.'

The two men squeezed in beside Joseph.

'How long is it since we met?' Prof said over his shoulder as he drove on.

'A long time,' said Lomunyak. 'Many years. It was when you came the first time to study the old places of our ancestors.'

Peter was looking at the three children with a puzzled frown.

'These are not all your children, Prof,' he said. 'One is African, one is *mzungu* and one is—'

'African *and mzungu*,' said Afra defensively. 'Prof's my dad. My mum was Ethiopian.'

'And we're her friends,' said Tom.

Joseph took a deep breath.

'*Lo murrani,*' he said shyly, trying out his first Maa greeting.

Peter smiled at him. 'Good. Very good. You are all welcome in Maasailand.'

'So,' said Prof. 'How are things, Lomunyak? What's the news?'

The older man shook his grizzled head.

'Things are not good. The drought is very bad. Many of our cattle have died. Look, can you see? The stream there, how small it is? Our people are suffering, really.'

Afra shifted restlessly in her seat.

'It's so awful,' she burst out suddenly, 'that all this—' she swept out an arm to embrace the vast panorama of Mountview Ranch, 'that all *this* belongs to one rich creep! One fat cat *mzungu* making heaps of money for himself! And outside it everyone else is just suffering!'

Peter and Lomunyak looked at each other, puzzled. Prof, looking in his mirror, saw the looks they exchanged.

'She says it is not good for one rich *mzungu* to have so much land and make a lot of money,' he said.

Peter and Lomunyak shook with laughter.

'John Grant?' said Peter, speaking in English

again. 'He does not make money from this land. How can he? It is not good for cattle. You can see it. The grass is thin. And this ranch is not a farm. It is a wildlife conservation trust. Before, the farmers tried to have cattle here, too many cattle, but in the drought time the cows eat everything, and the grass goes too fast. The cattle become very thin and then they die. The wild animals, they are not like the cattle. They eat some grass here, some leaves there, and then, if there is no grass, they go out to other places to find their food. Wild animals, they are very clever for finding their food.'

Afra frowned, as if she was about to say something else, but bit her lip and said nothing.

'That's migrating, isn't it?' said Tom, who was following Peter's heavily accented English with difficulty.

'Migration, yes. Animals from here, from Mountview, they are migrating all the time to the north, to our own Maasai ranch, and then coming back to Mountview again.'

Joseph turned and stared at Peter.

'*Your* ranch? You have a ranch?'

He couldn't believe that these men in their red *shukas* and old sandals made out of used car tyres could possibly own a ranch.

'Yes, of course we have a ranch,' said Lomunyak. 'It is very big, like Mountview. It is a group ranch for many Maasai people.'

'But don't your cattle eat all the grass and die, like they used to here at Mountview?' persisted Joseph. 'I thought Maasai people liked to have many cows.'

Lomunyak settled his red *shuka* more comfortably across his knees and his red and black bead bracelets flopped down onto his wrists. He patted Joseph kindly on the wrist.

'We have a small number of cattle only,' he said. 'We are like Mountview Ranch now. Our ranch is for wildlife.'

Peter nudged him and pointed out of the window.

'Look, rhino,' he said.

Everyone turned to look. A big male rhino was ambling across the stretch of grass below the track towards a clump of fever trees by the stream, where a pair of waterbuck, their shaggy heads lowered, were standing in the lush grass on the bank. The rhino's head was lowered and his small eyes, almost invisible in the thick creases of hide on his face, stared out myopically as he walked slowly, at a lumbering pace, through the brittle grass. He looked like the relic of a long gone prehistoric age.

'That is what we want. Rhino,' said Lomunyak, leaning forward, his sharp eyes assessing the rhino's size and strength. 'He is a good one. Look at his horns.'

Joseph withdrew his wrist. A horrible doubt

was creeping into his mind. Rhino horn was extremely valuable, he knew that. Poachers risked their lives for a chance to kill rhinos and steal their horns. He wanted to ask a question but he didn't know how to put it.

Afra got in first. Suspicion bristled in her voice. 'Why do you want rhinos on your ranch? To get their horns?'

Joseph clenched his fists with embarrassment as Peter and Lomunyak sucked in their breath with shocked disapproval. Prof turned to Afra with an angry frown on his face.

'No!' Peter's voice was fierce. 'Our rangers will shoot anyone, any poacher, who tries to take our game! If we have a rhino, we will look after him – oh, so much! It is true, before, we used to drive the wildlife away and think only of our cattle, but now we have changed our minds. We will do as our grandfathers did and live together with the wild animals. We want them to return to us. Slowly, slowly, they are coming back. Elephants have returned, and many gazelle and antelope. But rhinos, they are slow to move to a new place. And Grevy zebra, we want them too much also.'

'I don't understand,' said Tom. It was a tight squash in the back of the Land Rover and he was wriggling to get more comfortable. 'I mean, it's brilliant to have the wildlife around and every-thing, but how can you afford it? I mean, you can't get milk from them, or sell them or anything, like you can with cows.'

Peter laughed.

'You are clever, Tom. An economics student. No, we cannot buy or sell our wildlife, but it is very good for our prosperity. Tourists come to our lodge to see our animals. They pay us a lot of money. That is why we need the rare ones, like the rhino and the Grevy zebra. Tourists like too much to see them.'

'Tourists? You have a *tourist* lodge?' Joseph couldn't keep the incredulity out of his voice. He had seen posh tourist lodges in the national game parks. He just couldn't imagine Peter and Lomunyak, with their bare legs and long dangling earlobes serving cocktails and dishing up three course de luxe dinners to fussy foreign tourists.

He looked up and saw an understanding gleam in Peter's eyes. He felt embarrassed, afraid that his thoughts had shown too clearly on his face.

Peter leaned forward and tapped Prof on the shoulder.

'Prof,' he said. 'Send these children to us tomorrow, to Ol Tupesi. We will show them the most beautiful lodge in Africa. They can stay the night with us.'

Joseph, in the mirror, saw a smile spread across Prof's face.

'That's a great idea,' he said. 'If I get all you kids out of the way, maybe I can get some serious work done. Unless I can persuade you all to help out on the archaeological survey? No? OK. Ol Tupesi it is.'

They had arrived at the lodge at last. The Land Rover pulled up under the shade of a tree and they all spilled out.

'Come and have tea with us,' Prof said to Lomunyak.

He started off round the side of the lodge house.

'I'll make the tea, Prof,' said Afra, who was still smarting under Prof's disapproval, and wanted to make up for her rudeness. 'You all can sit down on the veranda and I'll bring it out to you.'

Joseph was leading the way. He had almost reached the low steps leading up to the veranda when he stopped so suddenly that the others nearly cannoned into him.

'Monkeys!' he whispered. 'Look!'

A troop of golden-haired vervet monkeys had been playing on the veranda. They saw Joseph and, nervously, bounded up the nearest tree. They were watching the humans uneasily, bobbing their startlingly black faces round first one side of the trunk, then the other.

Peter clapped his hands, and the monkeys scampered further away, chattering crossly.

'They are thieves,' Peter said. 'It is not good if they come to the house. They will bother you too much. Look.'

He went to the edge of the veranda and pointed down to the ground below. A piece of blue material lay crumpled on the ground, and some bright coins were scattered around it.

'My jacket!' said Tom indignantly, 'and the money that was in my pockets! I suppose I must have left it here when we went out this morning.'

He jumped down to retrieve it. The monkeys retreated reluctantly, watching his every move.

A few minutes later, Afra appeared with a heavily laden tray. She set it down on the table and began to pour milk and tea into the delicate white cups. Peter took his cup with a sideways glance at Lomunyak and spooned four teaspoons of sugar into it. Lomunyak, too busy to meet his eye, was doing the same.

They sat back, their cups in their hands, and sipped the hot sweet liquid. Lomunyak smiled guiltily.

'Tea, it is very nice,' he said. 'Our young warriors, they are giving us too much trouble because of it. They should eat only meat and drink only milk and blood, as our fathers did. Only in this way can they be healthy and strong, great Maasai warriors. But they like tea and sugar too much. Even when they are in the bush, training for battles, testing their strength against each other and practising with their spears, they come creeping home to the village to ask their mothers for tea.'

'You are right,' said Peter, shaking his head disapprovingly. 'Young people, they are weak. They are not as we were.'

Joseph felt a spurt of anger. He jumped up from the veranda rail where he had been perching and leaped away down the steps, taking them three at a time.

They're just stupid old men! he said savagely to himself. What do they know about young people? If we are no good, whose fault is it? Who is to blame?

4

THE LODGE AT OL TUPESI

The next morning, Prof dropped the three children off early at the main Mountview Ranch office, where a pick-up was about to leave for Ol Tupesi.

'Have a great time,' he said, as they jumped into the back seat. 'Come back in one piece.'

It was a long drive to Ol Tupesi, the Maasai group ranch, and the further they went the more Joseph became uneasy. Grandfather had often talked about the Maasai, about their daring, their fearsome skill with spears and their cattle rustling exploits.

'Maasai – very brave, very dangerous fellows,' he had frequently said, shaking his old head solemnly.

What with one thing and another, Joseph thought, this holiday hadn't turned out at all as he'd expected. He'd been away with Prof and Afra before, when Prof had gone out on archaeological field trips. They'd usually left Prof on his own to poke around on sites full of meaningless old stones and bits of bone, and had gone off to explore. Joseph had always wanted to come to this part of the country, with its wonderful animals and wide open spaces. But now he was here, he felt indifferent to everything.

I suppose it's nice here, he thought, watching out of the window as a lilac-breasted roller flew up into the air with a burst of speed, then rolled over in mid-flight to display its marvellous mauve and turquoise feathers.

But he couldn't summon up his old enthusiasm. He felt as hot and dried up inside as the parched and baking land all around.

Nothing ever goes right for me, he thought bitterly.

Now, racing along in this old pick-up on his way to an unknown ranch, run by a crowd of Maasai, he felt his heart sink even further. He didn't know these people.

I don't believe they've got a proper tourist lodge at all, thought Joseph anxiously. And if they try to make me drink any blood, I will refuse. I will definitely refuse.

Tom suddenly nudged him in the ribs.

'Wow,' he said. 'Look at that.'

The pick-up they were in turned with a flourish on a patch of bare earth and came to a halt, right in front of a ring of young warriors. They all wore the traditional red *shukas* and necklaces and bracelets of bright scarlet, blue, black and white beads, and Joseph's heart missed a beat as they crowded round the car.

The driver, who had said little during the journey and who, unlike the others, wore the dark green uniform of a ranger, leapt lightly down from the driver's seat. Afra, Tom and Joseph followed more slowly.

The tallest of the warriors, who seemed to Joseph to look down on him from an enormous height, came forward, smiling.

'I am Sipul,' he said. 'I am the manager of Ol Tupesi lodge.' He pointed to the shorter man standing beside him, whose cheekbones swelled out prominently over hollow cheeks. 'And this is Loipa. He is the deputy manager. Come, follow me.'

He turned, and began to run effortlessly up the steep hillside into what looked like a thicket of bushes.

'Eh, eh,' said Joseph under his breath. 'Where has Prof sent us to this time?'

Tom and Afra exchanged nervous looks, then Joseph, afraid more than anything else of seeming afraid, set off first up the steps after Sipul, painfully aware of the steel-like strength of the young man's rippling calf muscles ahead of him.

He came out at the top into a sight so unexpected that he gasped out loud.

A huge thatched roof, held up by thick tree trunks, had been built over a platform on the side of the hill. It was open all round the sides, and furnished with cushioned armchairs and low

coffee tables, on which lay bird books and bin-
oculars. At one end was a bar, and behind it stood
a warrior, holding a glass up in his hand.

'Juice?' he said invitingly to Joseph. 'Pepsi?
Fanta?'

Behind him, Joseph heard Tom and Afra reach
the top of the steps and gasp in turn. They
advanced into the cavernous open room and
looked around in wonder.

'It's like a cathedral or something,' said Tom.
'Only without any walls.'

'It's the best, just the *best*,' said Afra, sinking
down into one of the chairs.

In a moment she was up again.

'I don't believe this!' she cried. 'Just look at the
view!'

She came over to stand beside Joseph and Tom
and the three of them looked out over the deep
ravine below, through which a stream ran, feeding
a pool. Beyond it, the land flattened out. It was
covered with small scrubby trees and it stretched
for miles, away into the distance, where a fringe
of mountains formed the far horizon.

From somewhere down below came the unmistakable cracking, wrenching sound of a falling
tree.

'Elephants,' said Sipul with satisfaction. 'They
are knocking down a tree.'

Joseph looked round at him.

'You don't mind about that?' he asked, his eyes filled with surprise.

'No.' Sipul turned to see Loipa standing beside him, and he leaned his elbow on Loipa's shoulder. He was so tall, and Loipa was so short that they looked almost comical, and Afra had to stifle a giggle.

Sipul didn't notice. He was pointing out at the land.

'Look,' he said. 'Down there. Only poor shrubs, not good trees. These shrubs are just like weeds. They have grown quickly since the elephants left this place. They are not good for most kinds of wildlife. The zebras, for one, they need grass and other plants, and the grass will not grow until the scrub has gone. Some shrubs we will like to remain, because they will grow up to be big trees, and they will make shade, and a place for the birds, but the elephants will not destroy them all. When they have done their work, the land will be as it was before, good mixed land, some trees, some grass. It will be good for gazelle and many different kinds of animals.'

'Hey, I can see them!' called Tom. He was waving excitedly towards the stream. 'Look! Down there! Three – no, four elephants! They're the best. Elephants are just my best animals ever.'

Joseph was looking round the room. It was brilliant, one of the best places he'd ever seen, but he still couldn't quite believe that this was a proper lodge, with bedrooms and everything.

'Where are we going to sleep?' he asked Sipul. 'In here?'

Sipul laughed.

'No! Do you want to see your room? We will show you.'

The three children followed Sipul and Loipa to the back of the great room to a place where a path started up on a winding course around the side of the hill. Tucked in among the trees, almost invisible until you came upon it, was another vaulted thatched roof, smaller than the first. It too was open where the walls should have been, and under its cool shade stood three beds, swathed in new muslin mosquito nets. Behind a wall of rough hewn logs, in a corner of the room, was a perfect little bathroom.

Tom and Afra were running round in delight, touching everything and exclaiming loudly.

'You mean we're going to *sleep* here? Sort of in the open? Without any walls?'

Joseph wanted to join them, but an irritating little voice in his head was asking fearful questions.

Isn't it dangerous to sleep without walls? What if a robber comes? Or a leopard even?

He didn't say anything. He didn't want anyone to know he felt nervous.

Tom came to a halt suddenly, and asked the question out loud.

'Hey, is it safe here? Couldn't leopards and hyenas and lions and stuff get in and, you know, eat us in the night?'

Joseph felt an irrational prickle of irritation. Tom's question seemed crude, a little insulting even. But he was glad when Sipul jerked his head, indicating a man in a green uniform, a rifle over his shoulder, who had stepped silently into the room behind them.

'There is no danger,' said Sipul, and his calm confidence was reassuring. 'Our rangers are watching. Day and night they are guarding us.'

Afra was exploring the bathroom, picking up the soap and sniffing its perfume luxuriously.

'It's like a posh hotel or something,' she said. 'At least, I wouldn't know, because I've never stayed in one. Only it's much much better because it's right out here in the middle of nowhere.'

Tom was standing at the edge of the room, looking down into the ravine below.

'The elephants have gone,' he said. 'I wish we could go down there. It looks brilliant.'

'You want to go down to the river?' said Sipul. 'OK, we can go. If there is a ranger with us, we will be safe.'

He said a few words in Maa to the ranger, who nodded and began to lead the way out of the room again.

Joseph held back until he and Loipa, the short warrior, were the only ones still in the room.

'You want to go down, my brother?' asked Loipa.

Looking up, Joseph saw understanding in his eyes.

'Yes,' he said, smiling suddenly, and he began to run down the steps after the others.

It was a steep climb down to the floor of the ravine. While he was still going down, Joseph had to concentrate on the path, jumping down from rock to rock and slithering on the sandy bits, and he didn't take much note of the dry, drought-stricken vegetation around him. But when he came out on to the floor of the deep valley, where the stream whispered over smooth pebbles and rippled across undulating layers of fine sand, he looked around in amazement.

The world was suddenly fresh and green. Acacia trees spread their cool canopy overhead, while here and there the lush foliage of palms made a deeper shade. Their great fronds arched over gracefully, as light and feathery as an ostrich's pinions, and were reflected in the water of the pool that had been formed in a bend of the stream. Amongst the cawings and chirrupings of unseen birds came a sweet, repeated, bell-like song, and, even more loudly, the endless *shshsh* of a thousand crickets.

'You wouldn't know there was a drought here

at all,' said Tom, retrieving his foot from the mud at the water's edge, which was threatening to suck his shoe right off. 'What's that white thing over there?'

He was pointing to what seemed to be a block of weathered stone.

'It is salt,' said Sipul. 'Many animals like salt. They will come from many miles to lick it. With this salt, and the pool we have made, we are attracting new species all the time. They are safe here. They find what they need with us.'

Loipa had moved round the edge of the pool. He had squatted down, and was studying the ground with intense concentration.

Suddenly, he looked up, and beckoned urgently to the others. They ran over to him but before they had quite reached him he waved at them to stop. Looking down, Joseph saw that he was studying a maze of animal prints in the soft ground at the water's edge.

Joseph turned his head from one side to the other, trying to make sense of it all. He could pick out the cloven hooves of a waterbuck, and the huge footprints, as big as teatrays, that the elephants had made. Those little paw prints with sharp claw marks must be the tracks of a jackal, while the jumbled pattern of short lines, which made the ground look as wrinkled as an elephant's hide, must have been made by dozens of birds' feet.

Loipa was excitedly pointing something out to Sipul.

'*Ol-oitiko*!' he said. 'Zebra!'

Sipul squatted down beside him, then he looked up at Joseph and the others, a delighted smile on his face.

'Grevy zebra,' he said. 'A big stallion. This is our first to come here. It is very rare, very precious. Perhaps, if we are lucky, we will see him tonight if he comes again to drink.'

Loipa was on his feet now, moving away from the pool, his head down, following the tracks on the ground.

'That is not so good,' he grunted. 'Look, he is wounded. Here, and here. He is using one leg lightly only. He is pressing on the other legs.'

Joseph, remembering how Grandfather could read a whole history in the tracks of an animal, was staring at the ground intently himself. Suddenly he stopped. He had seen something imprinted on the soft earth, something large and unmistakable.

'Loipa!' he called out. 'Look at this! I'm not exactly sure, but I think – isn't it the mark of a lion?'

5

THE WARRIORS' SONG

For a moment, silence fell on the little group of people under the trees. Then Loipa and Sipul began to search further afield, looking for more tracks, and Joseph, Afra and Tom found themselves sidling closer together as if for protection.

'You don't think,' Tom said to Sipul, in a voice that was trying to sound brave, 'that it's around here somewhere at the moment, do you?'

Joseph could sense that Afra was listening as eagerly for the answer as he was.

Sipul glanced at the watch that nestled among the beaded bracelets on his wrist.

'No, it is too early. He will come to drink when the sun is setting, perhaps. But it is better for us to go up now, to the lodge.'

Loipa was already leading the way, running up the steep slope on winged feet. Joseph, who was used to running miles to his school in Nairobi every day, raced after him. He knew Tom would be at his heels, trying to keep up, but he didn't look round until he was nearly at the top. Then he turned, and saw with satisfaction that Tom was still some way behind, and that his face was scarlet with exertion.

Tom grinned at him as he reached the top.

'OK, you win. This time,' he said, and they both put up their right hands and slapped them together.

A group of nine or ten other warriors and rangers were waiting in the great reception room. They nodded respectfully as Sipul gave out a series of murmured instructions in Maa.

'What happens next?' said Afra, delighted anticipation in her face.

'It is our evening time soon,' said Sipul. 'Drink something. Rest for a while. Then we will show you.'

Joseph fetched himself a glass of water from the bar, sank down into one of the armchairs and let his eyes drift lazily over the view below. Behind him he could hear Tom and Afra playing a noisy game of cards. He didn't want to join them. He wanted to let his mind quieten down, to relax and empty itself of all the turbulence of the last two days.

He was nearly asleep, and the shadows outside were already lengthening, when Sipul came back.

'We are ready,' he said. 'Come.'

He led the way out of the huge room along another narrow path. The sinking sun had changed the colours of the whole world around them. At midday, the yellows and browns of the earth and trees and rocks had been bleached to a shimmering paleness by the sun at its blinding height, and every colour had been reduced to a faded, sandy dun. But now the whole land glowed in the golden light. The dry ground was a rich ochre, a lizard on a stone shone like a green jewel on a pewter dish, while overhead the sky was a deep heavenly blue, fading almost to indigo at the horizon.

'Where are we going? Where's he taking us?' whispered Tom.

Joseph didn't bother to answer. His anxiety had gone now. He trusted Sipul and Loipa completely.

They came out at last onto a flat rock from which the ground fell away steeply on one side. Two warriors were already there, piling branches on top of a bed of ashes, where fires had clearly been lit many times before. One of them struck a match and poked it into the dry grass and twigs in the centre, and the fire blazed up, catching the bigger branches and quickly settling into a steady, flaming glow.

Mesmerized, Joseph sat on a smooth stone nearby and watched the flickering tongues of flame. He felt a piercing sadness, as if he'd lost something infinitely precious, and at the same time an intense longing, though he didn't know what it was for.

Loipa shut his eyes and raised his chin. Then, starting in a voice almost too low to hear, that rose in a gathering volume of sound, he began to sing.

'What are the words? What does it mean?' Joseph whispered to Sipul.

Sipul, like the other warriors, was listening with pleasure, letting his hands flop to and fro in time to the rhythm, but he stood up and came close to where Joseph, Tom and Afra were sitting, and he sat down beside them, and translated in a low voice as the song went on.

'He is singing about a lion,' he said. 'And about other things. Here are the words:

Greetings to you, my comrades, my warriors!
Do you not know me?
I am your brother, and my cows are healthy.
My heifers are fat and my bulls are strong!
Did you not hear how a lion came once,
how he came to our resting place?
We took our spears, we drove him away!
His roar was loud, his teeth were long,
We did not fear him!
We will not fear him!
A zebra has come to our pool.
His stripes are thin and beautiful.
They are black and white together.
Lucky combination!
Welcome to our pool, beautiful zebra.
Stay with us.
We will drive the lion away.
He will never harm you.

Stay with us, beautiful zebra.
Stay with us!'

Loipa let the last note linger for a long moment, then the music died away. Joseph looked up at him.

The young man's eyes were fixed on the fire, and in the gathering darkness the light flickered on his dark brown gleaming chest. The other warriors lowered their heads and grunted their appreciation, but no one spoke. The music had woven a spell around them. No one wanted to break it.

Then Sipul leaned forward and pushed his fingers into the dry white ash at the edge of the fire. He went up to Loipa and drew white stripes on his bare brown arm. The other warriors, as if they had been released, jumped up and began to do the same to each other, making stripes of ash on their arms and faces.

The mood had changed. Exhilaration was sweeping round the little group, a rising tide of excitement. Everyone was standing now, and the warriors were beginning to shuffle and stamp their feet. Tom, infected with the mood, darted forward to the fire and caked his fingers with ash. Then he ran up to Joseph and began to draw stripes on his face.

Joseph stepped back involuntarily. He looked uneasily at the warriors, ready to be embarrassed, but they were laughing and slapping each other's backs, getting ready for their dance.

Joseph felt his face split open in a smile.

'Do it to me,' said Tom.

Afra was approaching already, a pile of ash in one cupped palm.

'It won't show up on you,' she said. 'You're too white.'

'It might,' said Tom, squinting down at his arms. 'I'm all sunburnt and dusty. Here, let me put some on you.'

They pranced round each other, laughing and pushing, daubing each other with ash.

The warriors had formed a circle around the fire. Sipul began to sing, in a hoarse, throaty voice. The others joined in with a kind of chant, their voices coming from deep inside their chests.

'*Uh, uhuh, uh, uhuh*!' they sang in rhythmic unison, as they began to dance.

Joseph, Tom and Afra fell silent and watched, but after only a few moments a strong warrior hand plucked at each of theirs, and they found themselves part of the ring, dancing with the others.

The dance had started quietly, but it was going fast and furiously now. The warriors moved as if they were one, their arms and shoulders shaking energetically, their feet stamping backwards and forwards in complicated rhythms. They sang and grunted and whooped together, as if with one voice.

Then Loipa ran into the middle of the circle. He began to jump, rising straight up to an astonishing height in the air as if his taut calves were springs. Higher and higher he went, while drops of sweat flew off his forehead. Then, with a final spectacular leap, he subsided and Sipul took his place.

The dancing went on. One by one, the warriors entered the ring to perform their amazing leaps, while the others danced around them, chanting and moving in perfect rhythm.

Joseph felt self-conscious at first. He kept falling over his feet, and he didn't know what to do with his arms. The dry ash on his face tickled and the heat of the fire was making him sweat. Looking sideways, he could see that Afra and Tom, were dancing awkwardly too, unable to catch the rhythm or follow the warriors' easy, fluid movements.

Bend your knees, Joseph told himself. Hop on one leg and then on the other. Lean sideways.

He couldn't do it. He was ready to give up.

The warriors were dancing faster. They were singing together in a crescendo of sound, and the performers in the circle were leaping ever higher, with the speed and effortlessness of birds. Something began to well up inside Joseph. He forgot to think about how he was dancing, and suddenly found he was doing it better. His feet were following the rhythm of their own accord. His arms and shoulders were shaking by themselves. The dance was holding him, possessing him, in a glorious delirium.

The longing he had felt all evening was breaking up out of his chest and rising into his head. As the dance came to a sudden climax, and the leaping and stamping stopped, realization came to him.

I want to be one of a band like them, he thought passionately. I want to have warrior blood brothers, so that I would be part of them, and they'd be part of me. And we'd go into battle together, and fight for each other, and be friends till death, all of us.

The dancing stopped. The warriors laughed and clapped hands together, and began to disappear down the path towards the lodge. Loipa was busy trampling down the fire, heaping sand over it till not one spark was left.

Afra and Tom had collapsed in a heap against the rock.

'That was incredible,' said Afra. 'You're such a brilliant dancer, Joseph. I wish I could dance like you.'

'Yeah. You're the best,' said Tom enviously.

Joseph looked from one to the other. Even though it was almost dark now that the fire had been put out, he could see the smiles on their faces and hear the warmth in their voices.

This is what I have, he thought with surprise. Afra and Tom aren't my blood brothers, they could never be that. But they're my friends. My best friends.

Sipul was starting out up the path.

'Come!' he called back to them. 'It is time for supper. We have prepared very nice food for you. Some roasted meat and some chips.'

'Chips!' said Tom. 'Brilliant! We thought we'd have to drink—'

'Sh!' said Joseph, digging him in the ribs, and giggling, the three of them followed Sipul up the path to the lodge.

6

CAMEL RIDE

It was eerie but fun going to bed in the open-sided room. Joseph was the last to get ready. He turned the light out and made a dive for his bed. He tucked the mosquito net securely all round him and lay on his back, looking at the shadows which the rising moon was casting on the under-side of the thatched roof. They seemed to move ominously. He was glad he was enclosed in the soft white net. It was no more than a piece of flimsy material, but it felt safe inside nevertheless. It was like being swathed in a protective cocoon.

'I'm going to make myself a house like this one day,' said Tom happily. 'It'll be on a hill, just like this one, and you'd be able to see out for miles and miles. I'll make it myself out of bits of wood and thatch and stuff, just a roof, without walls or doors or anything.'

'Sounds cool,' said Afra. 'I'll come and stay. But what about water and electricity? You have to have those.'

'I'd make it near a stream, like Ol Tupesi, and have solar panels, like they've got here. And I'd have it right under a tree with a kind of rope

57

ladder going up, so if anyone came who I didn't want to see, I could just get up into the tree and pull the rope ladder up and they wouldn't even know I was there.'

'Like early humans,' said Afra. 'I bet that's what they did. Made their houses near trees. There were all kinds of much worse predators around then. Sabre-toothed tigers and things like that.'

'You could easily do it, you know,' said Tom. 'Live right out in the wild, I mean, and eat roots and berries and small game and stuff. And all you'd need is a satellite phone and a solar powered computer and you'd be able to link yourself up onto the internet.' He paused. 'I'd get a bit lonely though. I'd miss Mum and Dad and Jimmy and everyone. And the people from school. Some of them, anyway.'

'I wouldn't miss anyone at all, except for you two, and Prof, a bit.' Afra sounded wistful. 'I'd love it. Living right out here in the bush! Think of all the animals you'd see, once they were used to you. You'd really get to know them and sort of live with them. They'd end up totally accepting you.'

Joseph listened without joining in.

They're like little kids, he thought. They don't know what they're talking about. People in Africa have always lived out in the wild and made their own houses and found their own food. Grandfather did. The Maasai do. And it's a hard life, and there's never enough to eat, and there are dangerous animals, and it's really scary.

Aloud he said, 'It's not so wonderful living in a little house you make yourself. It's all dark and smoky and the rain comes in. I'm going to get a builder to build a house for me one day. In Nairobi. It'll have lots of rooms, and beautiful furniture, and one room just for table tennis, and a special lovely one for my goat.'

No one spoke for a moment. Then Afra said dreamily, 'And a garden with huge trees full of birds and monkeys.'

'And a games room,' said Tom, 'with a computer, and loads of TVs so you can watch six football games all at once.'

'That's so boring, Tom,' Afra yawned. 'Couldn't we have a nice muddy pool where elephants could wallow instead?'

'Afra, you're not bringing any elephants into *my* house,' said Joseph, 'and that is final.' There was a pause. 'And there'd be the biggest freezer in the world,' he went on, 'full of mango ice cream.'

'Sounds like a palace to me,' said Afra.

'It will be,' said Joseph drowsily. 'You'll see.'

He woke just after dawn. The bullfrogs, which had been croaking loudly in the pool below the night before, were quiet now, but a noisy crow was cawing on the roof overhead.

It's never silent out in the bush, Joseph thought.

He pulled up his mosquito net and jumped out of bed. The big room looked smaller by daylight. The shadows that had seemed to move in the moonlight were motionless now.

He padded barefoot over to the edge of the room and looked out. A palm frond in the valley below was waving about while the rest of the tree was still. Was it a freak gust of wind, or was a bird or a monkey or a snake moving there? At any rate, there was no sign of human habitation as far as he could see.

Even if my father goes to Mountview Ranch to look for me, he'll never come out this far, thought Joseph, with a mixture of relief and regret.

The sun was rising with almost visible speed. Its warmth seemed to soothe the night's restlessness. The cool breeze was dropping, and the birds were quietening down. In the place of their strenuous song came the leisurely droning of a bee. Joseph could hear murmured voices now too, and the clink of utensils as the warriors, in the cookhouse further round the hillside, were lighting the fire and getting breakfast ready.

Then, over all the other sounds, Joseph heard a new one. It began as a roar, a kind of wild bellow, and it ended suddenly on a laughing note, like a donkey's bray.

The warriors had clearly heard it too. The clattering of dishes stopped, and their voices were raised in excitement.

'*Ol-oitiko*!' Joseph heard them say, one after the other.

Afra and Tom were stirring behind him.

'What was that noise?' asked Afra sleepily.

'The Grevy zebra I think,' said Joseph, who was craning his neck as he looked down the hill, hoping to see a flash of black and white stripes.

Afra was in the bathroom already, pulling on her clothes, and Joseph and Tom hurried into theirs. They took the steps on the path out of their room three at a time, and burst into the cookhouse.

'Was it? Was it the Grevy stallion?' panted Afra.

'Yes!' said Loipa, who was supervising the cooking. 'It cannot be another animal. Only the Grevy can make this sound.'

'What's the matter, Loipa?' said Tom. 'You don't look too happy.'

'The stallion is wounded, we think.' An anxious crease was splitting Loipa's forehead. 'When he roars in this way, the lions can hear him. They will be attracted to him, perhaps. Lions, they like zebra meat too much.'

'What are you going to do?' said Afra.

'We will go out now and look for him. If we can protect him from the lions, it is good. Also, if his wound has become infected, perhaps we can get medicine for him.'

'We'll come and help,' said Tom. 'Can we?'

Loipa looked at him doubtfully.

'You are not afraid of lions?'

Tom drew a deep breath.

'Not – not much. Not if you aren't.'

Loipa looked over Tom's head to Joseph.

'And you?'

Joseph saw a challenge in his eyes and nodded.

'I'll come.'

'And if you think you're all going off without me, you can think again,' said Afra. 'Don't even try to suggest it. I mean, that would just be so outrageous, I'd – I'd—'

Loipa pursed his lips.

'You can be quiet?' he said. 'You can stay silent for a long time without talking?'

'What do you take me for?' began Afra indignantly. 'Of course I—'

Tom started coughing meaningfully and Joseph joined in. Their chorus of coughs turned into cackles of laughter.

'Don't listen to them, Loipa,' said Afra, turning her back ostentatiously on the two boys. 'They're just a couple of dumb kids. But I can make them stay quiet. I'll just keep my eye on them for you and make sure they shut up.'

Joseph and Tom stopped laughing and stared at her.

'You *what*?' said Tom.

'Afra, you . . . you—' spluttered Joseph.

'When do you want to start?' said Afra, smiling sweetly at them, then gazing innocently up at Loipa. 'Now? I'm ready. I guess the boys might need a little longer to get themselves organized.'

'No, no,' said Loipa, smiling understandingly at Joseph's and Tom's outraged faces. 'We must have our breakfast first, and wait for the rangers to come. They will bring the camels.'

'Camels?' Tom and Afra said together.

'Yes. It is better to go with camels. You will ride on them and look down from above. You will see further that way. And then, if there is some danger, from an elephant perhaps, you can escape more quickly. The camels, they can run very fast.'

'If you manage to stay on,' said Tom doubtfully.

Joseph felt his stomach lurch with fear. He had never ridden a camel before. He was afraid he'd make a fool of himself in front of the others, fall off his camel, maybe, or let it run away. And he was, he had to admit it, really afraid of lions.

Loipa shooed them out of the cookhouse, up to the great reception room, and a few minutes later Sipul called them in to breakfast.

Joseph sat down to a big plateful of eggs and bacon and a cup of steaming tea. He didn't look up. He didn't want them to sense his foreboding.

They ate in silence, sipping their tea slowly as if to put off the moment of departure.

'I'm scared,' said Afra at last. 'I haven't ridden a camel before. And there are lions about.'

Joseph was grateful to her for saying it first.

'I'm scared too,' he admitted.

'And me,' said Tom.

Before they had a chance to say anything else, Loipa came back with a ranger.

'The camels are here. Are you ready?' he said.

Joseph stood up first.

'Yes, we're ready.'

He followed Loipa down the steps to the place where the pick-up was still parked at the bottom of the hill. Three camels, already saddled, were waiting patiently, their noses in the air, their thickly lashed brown eyes seeming to gaze contemptuously down at the humans below. Two rangers held their bridles.

Afra bent to examine the camels' bellies.

'What are you doing?' Joseph asked curiously.

'Just making sure the girths aren't too tight,' she said. 'I couldn't bear for us to hurt them.'

One of the rangers gave a low command and jerked on the lead camel's bridle. Protesting with loud growling noises, the camel sank down onto his knees. The other two did the same.

Joseph climbed gingerly onto his camel, and at once the big animal began to rise, bucking Joseph backwards and tossing him forwards again.

Joseph held on tight, forcing himself to smile down at the others.

'It's OK,' he said. 'No problem.'

It wasn't bad, in fact. The saddle was comfortable, and felt solid. The camel's sides were warm against his calves, and gave off a sweet, dusty smell. And Sipul had been right. The view was much better from this height. He could see over the bushes and small trees way off into the distance.

'Come on,' he called out to the others. 'Don't be scared. This is going to be great!'

7

ON THE TRAIL OF THE ZEBRA

The hill on which Ol Tupesi lodge had been built was part of a long escarpment that rose abruptly from the flat plain below. The little train of people and camels set off from the foot of the cliff, branching out into the arid wilderness of scrubby trees and bushes.

A ranger in a green uniform was leading the camels, and Loipa, with Boniface, another young warrior, was walking alongside. Sipul had stayed behind. Joseph had felt a little shock of disappointment. There was something reassuring about Sipul, with his calm confidence and his magnificent height.

Loipa's nice, he thought, glancing down to where Loipa, whose short legs gave him an oddly gangling gait, was walking along beside his camel. It's easy to get to know him. Perhaps he is a little like me.

Riding a camel wasn't too difficult. It was more relaxed and comfortable than Joseph had expected. The alarming part was being perched right up on the camel's hump, so high above the ground, but once he was used to that, Joseph began to enjoy the swaying, rolling rhythm of the camel's stride.

In front of him was the back of Afra's camel, and beyond her was Tom's. They were both concentrating too hard on getting used to riding to turn and talk to him. With their wide-brimmed hats they looked like explorers from an earlier age.

Joseph felt uncomfortable. It seemed wrong that he, Tom and Afra were riding, while Loipa, Boniface and the ranger had to walk.

'Do you want me to get off?' he asked Loipa awkwardly. 'Would you like to ride?'

Joseph saw Loipa's hollow cheeks crease as he smiled.

'No. Perhaps later. The camels are scared sometimes. We know them. It is better for us to lead them.'

'Oh.'

Joseph's hands tightened on the pommel of his saddle, betraying his own nervousness. He made himself look up. He could see from here how bad the drought was. Deep fissures criss-crossed the cracked earth, leaves had withered on the trees, and here and there lay a pile of bleached bones, the remains of a starved cow.

All at once, he caught a movement not far away. It looked for a second like a zebra.

'I can see something!' he called out excitedly. 'Over there!'

Boniface turned. He had a round, friendly face that suited his name.

'It is the zebra?'

Joseph subsided back onto his saddle.

'No, sorry. It's only a shepherd boy with some goats. I thought for a moment it was – something else.'

He stopped, embarrassed. He could see the goats quite clearly now. One or two of them were pure white, and as they'd moved through the trees, the shadows and the intervening branches had given Joseph the illusion of stripes.

Tom's camel, up ahead, was already among the flock of goats. The ranger brought it to a halt, and the other camels stopped too.

A boy, only a little younger than Joseph, came running out from among the trees, a switch in his hand, and skidded to a halt, looking up curiously at the three children riding high above him on their camels. Then he saw Loipa, and an apprehensive look came into his eye. He looked curiously up at Joseph again. Joseph couldn't read his expression, but it made him feel uncomfortable.

'What's your name?' he said in Swahili, to break the silence.

'Lawrence,' said the boy.

'How many goats do you have?'

'Ten.'

Joseph ran out of questions. The boy saw that

his goats were scattering. He ran after them, shouting hoarsely, herding them back into a single flock. Then he came back, as if fascinated by Joseph, and stared up at him.

'Do you go to school?' he asked shyly.

Joseph nodded.

'Do you?'

The boy hitched up his tattered shorts, which were several sizes too big and hung loosely round his slim waist.

'I want to go, but my father forces me to look after the goats.'

'How does he force you?'

The boy shrugged.

'He beats me if I refuse.'

Joseph nodded sympathetically. Encouraged, the boy came closer.

'Can you read?' he asked.

'Yes.'

Joseph thought briefly of his big school in Nairobi, of the hordes of boys in their maroon and khaki uniforms, of the lessons and teachers, the homework and exams, the cheering boys at school football matches, the racket that followed the bell at the end of lessons. He was suddenly aware of how quiet it was here. The only sounds were the scrabbling of goats' hooves on the ground, and the soft nibbling of the camels as they browsed on the nearest withered bush.

'What do you do all day?' he asked the boy.

Lawrence shrugged. He was shooting uneasy glances at Loipa, who was talking in rapid Maa to Boniface and the ranger.

'When my brother is with me, we wrestle sometimes, and build little houses. But I have to look after the goats. I have to watch them all the time.'

Joseph nodded understandingly.

'I know. I have a goat at home in Nairobi.'

'Who looks after it when you go to school?'

'My mother.'

Lawrence looked surprised.

'Your mother? She doesn't mind?'

Joseph made a face.

'Yes, she does. You know what goats are like. Mine is brown. He's really beautiful but he eats everything. Even my clothes.'

Tom hadn't been able to understand the fast Swahili conversation. He was waiting impatiently for Joseph and Lawrence to stop talking, and as soon as they did, he said, 'Has he seen him, the Grevy stallion, I mean?'

Joseph translated the question. Lawrence shook his head.

'No, but I heard him, I think. Does he sound like this?'

He lifted his head, opened his mouth, and gave voice to a perfect copy of the stallion's roar. The camels started, and bent their heads disapprovingly.

'Yeah, that's it exactly,' said Afra.

'It's brilliant,' said Tom. 'Do it again.'

'No, that is enough!'

Loipa came up to Lawrence. His face was stern and unsmiling. He spoke to him sharply in Maa. Lawrence drew in his breath, and turning his flock around as fast as he could, he began to chase them back in the direction from which he'd come without a backward glance.

'What did you say to him?' Joseph asked curiously.

Loipa was looking annoyed. He jerked the bridle of Tom's camel, urging it on again.

'I have told him there is a lion here. It is hungry and it likes to eat goats. He must take his animals far away, or they will be eaten, and he will be eaten also. And, if he comes back to this place again, I will tell his father and he will be beaten.'

Afra looked round at him, a frown on her face. 'Why? Why do you want to get rid of him?'

Loipa was still looking angry.

'The boys here know well that goats are not allowed in this place. The elders of all the villages have agreed. In this part of the ranch we will encourage our wildlife, for the good of all our community. We do not want boys disturbing the animals, and goats eating all the grass and leaves. This boy, he has come here before. Boniface was telling me that he has warned him many times. He is too naughty, but this is his last chance.'

The cavalcade moved on. Joseph could still see

71

the goats, trotting away through the bushes, with the ragged figure of Lawrence, waving his stick and urging them along.

That would be me if I'd stayed in the village with Grandfather, he thought, and his feelings took another turning. Yesterday, he'd been angry that he'd had to spend his whole life in Nairobi. He'd envied the warriors, and their freedom, and their loyalty to each other. But I'd hate it, he told himself. I'd hate to be that boy. He must be lonely, and get bored, and be so scared when the lions come.

He shivered at the thought of lions, and looked round uneasily, but everything looked quiet and normal, the bushes still and the birds silent.

He went back to his nagging thoughts. He felt confused. He was being pulled in different directions.

I don't even know who I am, really, he thought. There was an emptiness inside him which frightened him. He'd felt it before, sometimes, but this was the worst he'd ever known. He was suddenly unsure where the edges of himself were, where he stopped and the rest of the world began.

Ahead of him, he was vaguely aware of Tom's and Afra's camels, moving steadily on.

Tom wouldn't understand anything like this, Joseph thought, feeling momentarily resentful of his friend. Afra might. Yes, Afra might.

He'd been too wrapped up in his thoughts to

notice what was happening, but Loipa had twitched at his camel's bridle and the camel had halted. Ahead, the others had stopped too. Loipa looked up and laid a warning finger on his lips.

Joseph's fear returned in a rush. What were Boniface and the ranger staring at so intently through the bushes in front?

Then, above the trees and bushes, he saw a moving grey bulk and his heart missed a beat. Elephants! There were elephants ahead!

He and Tom had encountered elephants before. They'd experienced their rage and seen the terror they had brought to a village. He could feel that terror again, now, in the pit of his stomach.

He couldn't understand why the ranger, Boniface and Loipa were waiting so calmly, why they hadn't turned round, why they weren't fleeing for the safety of the cliffs.

He could see three elephants now. No, four! He shrank down onto his saddle, trying to make himself as small as possible. The huge beasts were walking at a steady pace, cutting diagonally across the path, moving slowly away towards the pool below the lodge. Joseph began to breathe more easily. The elephants were clearly uninterested in the humans, although by now they must have smelled and heard the people and the camels.

He watched the last grey rump sway away out of sight and looked down at Loipa.

'You are not scared of them at all?'

Loipa tossed his head dismissively.

'The elephants here, they are very peaceful. We are not chasing them or making fires to drive them away. We do not hurt them and they do not hurt us. It is not necessary for us to be afraid.'

But I'm afraid all the time, Joseph thought unhappily. I'm scared of elephants and lions, and of people laughing at me, and of feeling empty. Of not knowing where I belong.

Loipa and Boniface had been conferring again. They called to the ranger, and at a signal from him, the lead camel dropped to its knees, almost unseating Tom, then settled with a groan onto its haunches. The other two camels did the same.

Joseph slithered down off his camel. He was glad to be back on solid ground again.

'Why did we stop?' Afra asked Loipa.

'We will wait here until the elephants are far away,' Loipa said. 'They are not so interested in us, but it is better to be sure. And there is a good place quite near to here, if we climb a little way. We can see very far into the distance. We can look for the zebra very well there.'

Tom came up, slapping the dust off his trousers.

'That was the best. Anyone got any biscuits? I'm hungry.'

'You can't be!' Afra looked revolted. 'You ate about half a ton of breakfast only an hour ago.'

Joseph, following Loipa as he climbed up onto

an outcrop of tumbled rocks, heard them bickering cheerfully behind him. He would have joined in usually, enjoying their teasing and silliness, but he didn't want to today. He felt miles away from them, from everyone, in fact.

He reached the top just after Loipa. Loipa bent down to push aside a dead branch covered with sharp thorns which lay across the rock, threatening to trip up anyone who crossed it, so it was Joseph who saw the zebra first.

'Yes! There!' he said in a hoarse whisper, grabbing Loipa's arm and pointing with a quivering finger to an open space on the far side of the rocks. 'Just there! That's him, isn't it? That's the Grevy stallion!'

8

THE LONELY STALLION

The stallion was some distance away. He was standing still with his head up, as if something had alerted him. Joseph, sinking down cautiously beside the others, felt a little breeze on his face.

He won't catch our scent, he thought with satisfaction. The wind's coming from him to us.

The zebra waited for a moment, then, seemingly reassured, he began to walk on towards where the camels were tethered at the foot of the rocks. He stopped and sniffed the ground, lifted his tail and released a few oval pellets of dung. Then he raised his head, stretched out his neck and gave tongue to another proud roar, which ended in an almost comical hee-haw.

Beside him, Joseph heard Loipa grunt with satisfaction.

'Good, that is very good,' he whispered. 'Did you see his dung? He is marking his territory. That means he wishes to remain here.'

'Why is he braying like that?' Joseph asked quietly. 'Is he feeling pain?'

'No. He is calling to other zebras, to the females. "Come into my territory," he is saying, "so that I can mate with you." He has a nice new home. He thinks the ladies will come to him.' A deep laugh rumbled in Loipa's throat. 'I hope he will be more lucky than me.'

The zebra was walking on again, coming closer and closer. Joseph could see him clearly now. He was a magnificent animal. His close-packed narrow stripes shimmered in the heat haze. They seemed to dance before Joseph's eyes. On his face, the stripes formed a diamond pattern. A black line underscored each eye, and his nose was a creamy white colour.

'Weird ears,' whispered Tom. 'Like Mickey Mouse.'

Joseph could see what Tom meant. The zebra's ears were round, sticking up out of his head like a pair of soup spoons. Bristly dark brown hair sprouted between them and ran on down the back of his neck to make a mane like a Mohican crest. The mane made a divide between the patterns of stripes on each of his flanks, and gradually diminished till it turned into a dark brown stripe, which ran all the way along his spine and ended in an arrow point halfway down his pale cream tail, from which a black tuft sprouted at the end.

'Beautiful,' breathed Afra. 'He's so beautiful.'

'He is *sedai*,' said Boniface. 'Lucky. In Maasai culture, black and white together is lucky.'

'Is it?' said Afra, looking pleased.

The zebra was very close now. He seemed

unaware of the watching humans. He stopped his stately progress, twitched his strange ears, shook his head and dropped it to the ground to nibble on a patch of dead yellow grass. As he turned, Joseph caught sight of an ugly wound running down his rump into his back right leg.

'Look there,' he whispered to Loipa. 'You were right. He *is* hurt. I can see it.'

Loipa and Boniface were observing the zebra carefully.

'It is not so bad,' murmured Boniface. 'It is not bleeding. I cannot see a swelling there.'

The zebra moved on. He was walking away from them now.

'But he can't live here alone, can he?' said Tom. 'I mean, don't they usually go in herds?'

'The common zebras go like that,' said Loipa. 'They are together in families, mares and stallions. But the Grevy, they are different. The females and foals, they stay together in a little herd but there are no males with them. The female herds, they wander about, here and there, and when the rains come, they think, "It is time to meet up with the guys," and they listen for this fellow to roar. Then they come to his territory. Only to inspect. If they like him, if he is big and strong and beautiful—'

'Like me,' said Boniface, adjusting the bright bangles on his wrist.

'You mean like *me*,' said Loipa, grinning and

puffing out his chest, 'they will stay with him and he will mate them.'

'So the mares and foals go to the stallions, do they?' Joseph was frowning over this.

'Yes. It is like people. The fathers, they are the ones to go out and find a new place. Then they call to the wife and kids to come.'

'Not always,' said Afra, bridling. 'Loads of women go off and explore too.'

And men aren't like zebras, thought Joseph bitterly. They go off and never bother to come back.

'Hey,' broke in Tom suddenly. 'Where's he gone? Look, he's just sort of vanished.'

He was screwing his eyes up against the light, staring in the direction where the zebra had gone.

Loipa laughed.

'No, he is there,' he said. 'Can't you see him? Under the tree.'

Joseph tried to focus his eyes, but the sun was so high now that the light was blinding. All he could see was the shimmering yellow grass, the long dry stalks rippling in the breeze.

Then, in the shade of the tree, he saw something white jerk up and down and realized it was the zebra's nose. At once, the rest of the zebra's body snapped into focus.

'Is that why they have stripes?' he asked Loipa. 'For camouflage?'

'Maybe. I do not know.' Loipa, who had been squatting on a flat rock, shifted his weight,

79

knocking his spear with his foot. 'There is something so wonderful about zebras. Every one is different! Did you know that? Every zebra has his pattern, not like the others.'

'You mean sort of like our fingerprints?' said Tom.

'Yes. And the baby, when he is born, the mother takes him away, far from the herd, so he can see only her stripes. Then he will learn she is his mother, and he cannot confuse her with the other mares.'

'Imprinting,' said Afra, grandly. 'Geese do it. The first moving thing they see when they're born, they think is their mom, and they just follow it around. I have a goose at home called Stumpy, and he's imprinted on me.'

'But what happens if the mares never find out that the stallion's here?' said Joseph. 'I mean, they might never come, and he could just stay here for ever, alone, marking his territory and roaring for no purpose. Just waiting for them to come.'

'You are right, Joseph.' Loipa stood up again and stretched his legs. The others did the same. 'But what can we do? If they come, they will come.'

'I wonder where this big guy came from,' said Afra, staring at the distant shadow under the tree. 'Is he still there? Yes, I just saw him twitch his tail. And there's another thing. How did he get that horrible wound?'

'It was from a spear, I think.' Boniface frowned with disapproval. 'He has come from the North, not from Mountview. Some people there, they like to hunt Grevy zebra for their meat. It is a bad drought in their place. Their cattle are dying.'

'That's terrible,' said Afra passionately. 'To kill something so beautiful! So *rare*! And just for a load of hamburgers. It's horrible!'

Loipa snapped his fingers irritably, but his voice was as calm as usual.

'It is horrible when your children are hungry,' he said. 'Meat is the only thing they desire. What does the word "rare" mean then?'

Afra was silent for a moment. Then she said, 'There might be other Grevys out there then, in danger! This guy was so lucky he found his way here, to the very place where he can be safe from people. Protected from lions, even! If only we could get the others to come here too. Isn't there some way we could do it? Attract them here, I mean?'

Boniface was already heading back down the rocks towards the camels below. Loipa picked his spear up and pointed with it out across the land. Joseph screwed up his eyes to look out too.

'The best we can do is to have a place like this, where the zebras will like to come. They need to be safe, away from poachers and from lions. We have done this. We have our rangers to protect them. All the time they are patrolling our borders, gathering information from our neighbours. Our people here, in our lands, they know how precious the Grevy are to us, for our future. They will never harm them.'

'OK.' Afra was tapping a foot briskly on the rock. 'But *they* won't know that, the zebras I mean. They don't know they'll be safe if they come here.'

'They will come for other reasons.' Loipa jerked his chin towards the distant green trees that marked the course of the stream. 'They will come for water. They can smell it from afar. And the salt, once they find the salt, they will come back and back to lick it.'

'The pool,' nodded Tom. 'That's such a brilliant place. I bet they love the pool.'

Joseph wasn't listening. He had seen in the far distance a moving line of dust billowing up from the ground. At the head of it, something glinted in the sun.

'A car's coming,' he said.

Loipa looked up briefly.

'It is our driver returning from Isiolo, with our supplies,' he said without interest.

'The pool's quite small, though, isn't it?' Tom was still following the same train of thought. 'I mean, when you think of all the animals, the elephants and waterbuck and everything, even the lions, it would be better if it was bigger, wouldn't it?'

He was scrambling back down the rocks now after Boniface.

'It will be bigger,' said Loipa, 'when the rains come. It will be better then. Everything will be better when the rains come.'

Joseph was the last to go down. He looked for one last time towards the shady tree. Was the zebra still there? He couldn't quite be sure.

Below him, Afra, who was nearly at the bottom of the climb, momentarily missed her footing and almost fell. She gave a sharp scream. The sound resonated into the distance, and Joseph knew that in the scrubby wilderness dozens of furry ears, some spotted, some striped, some brown, some grey, had heard the noise.

Humans, their owners would be thinking. Danger.

But some, Joseph thought, might be thinking, 'Food'.

It was funny how they had all forgotten about the lion. It seemed so quiet and normal down there. But he was around somewhere.

And I bet he knows where we are, Joseph murmured under his breath.

He looked round for one last time. The vehicle in the distance was still there. He could see it more clearly now. It was approaching fast, careering down the track towards Ol Tupesi. From below, Joseph heard a groan from Afra's camel as she began to mount it, and he quickly scrambled down the rocks to join the others.

'We found the zebra. What do we do now?' he asked Loipa.

Loipa looked questioningly from him to Tom and Afra.

'You would like to go further? To look out in case we find other zebras? But I do not think we will find any more. Perhaps we are ready to go back to the lodge and eat some lunch. Then you can take your rest beside the swimming pool.'

'A swimming pool? Is there a swimming pool at Ol Tupesi? We didn't know about that,' said Joseph.

Loipa looked surprised.

'There is a beautiful one! Sipul did not show you?'

'He hardly had time,' said Afra. 'We all went out singing and dancing last night, remember?'

Tom was fanning his face with his hat.

'A swim would be fantastic,' he said. 'I'm all hot and sticky and sweaty. What do you reckon, Joseph?'

Joseph didn't hear him. He was listening to the sound of the car, which was coming closer and closer.

'I guess we ought to go on just to check in case there are any other Grevys out there,' Afra began. Then she changed her mind suddenly. 'But hey, you're right, Tom. It's too hot now. And a swim sounds too good to be true. OK, Loipa, let's go home. Lunch and a swim win out, I guess.'

Tom had already mounted his camel and it was lurching to its feet. Joseph was about to follow when Loipa lifted his hand.

'The car,' he said. 'That is strange. It is not going to the lodge. It is coming this way.'

Everyone stopped to listen to the approaching car. All of a sudden it appeared through the scrub. It was an old white Toyota and it was approaching fast, weaving in and out between the trees.

'That is not our Ol Tupesi car,' Loipa said with a quick frown. He nodded to the ranger, who pulled his rifle down from his shoulder and held it ready in front of him.

Joseph's heart was beginning to flutter wildly.

What will I do if it's him? he thought. What will I say?

He turned his head from side to side, looking for a bolthole in the bushes nearby, but his feet seemed locked to the ground and he was unable to move.

The car driver saw them when he was nearly on top of them. He lurched to a halt but then sat, motionless, in the driving seat, looking straight ahead as if he didn't know what to do.

The ranger saw that Sipul was sitting in the passenger seat beside him, and hoisted his gun back up on his shoulder again. As if reluctantly, the driver opened the door of the car and jumped out. Joseph, his eyes clouded with panic, saw a burly man, shorter than he remembered, with no hair where there had once been a thick mat on the top of his head. He was standing by the car door, looking uneasily at each person in turn as if he was searching for someone.

Sipul was already coming around from the passenger seat, a big smile on his face.

'Joseph, here is a surprise for you!' he cried. 'Your father has come!'

9

LIONESS!

The years fell away from Joseph. He was a little boy of five again. An almost forgotten sensation, a mixture of helpless fear, anger and pure distress, engulfed him. His knees felt weak and his stomach churned.

Kioko Mutua had seen him now. He was looking puzzled, as if he was trying to trace the features of the little boy he'd left behind in the face of this tall youth.

'Joseph?' he said, in the deep, gravelly voice that had so often struck fear into Joseph's heart.

Loipa, trying to be helpful, dragged Joseph forward.

'Are you too shy to greet your own father?' he said.

Boniface had urged Tom's and Afra's camels to kneel again. They'd both dismounted, and were standing awkwardly nearby, looking curiously from Kioko to Joseph and back again, not knowing what to do.

Joseph looked into his father's face. Kioko wasn't smiling. His eyes were solemn. He was looking Joseph up and down, nodding with tense little motions of his head.

Sipul, watching them, withdrew some way away, and squatted down in the shade of a nearby tree. He signalled to the others and they went over to join him, tactfully turning their backs on Joseph and his father.

Kioko passed his tongue over his dry lips. Joseph's initial fright was beginning to wear off. His father was so much shorter than he remembered, so much less impressive.

I'm almost as tall as he is, he thought.

For years he'd framed in his head the questions he would ask his father. Where did you go? Why didn't you ever write to Mama? How could you abandon us? Didn't you care for us at all? Did you ever, once, think about me?

He'd forgotten all his questions now. The formidable, frightening man he'd carried in his head was quite different from the balding, almost insignificant figure in front of him.

Neither of them had said a word yet. Kioko broke the silence first.

'You are a good student? You are going to school?'

Joseph had dropped his eyes to the ground, but the harshness of the question made him jerk his head back.

'Yes,' he said, glancing at his father's eyes and looking away again.

He had an odd, momentary feeling that his father was embarrassed.

'You are still living in Nairobi? In Professor Tovey's house?'

Joseph nodded.

'That's Afra, over there,' he said unwillingly, jerking his head towards the group sitting under the tree.

'I saw Professor at Mountview. He told me you were here.'

Mama, Joseph was thinking. Why doesn't he ask about Mama?

Silence had fallen between them again.

'Your sister Monica, she is married?'

'Yes.' Joseph felt his lips compress to a thin line. He remembered how Mama had worked and saved to pay for Monica's wedding.

'Where's that husband of yours?' everyone had asked her. 'It's a good thing you have a son to look after you, eh, Joseph?'

Mama had laughed and smiled, keeping her anger and pain inside.

'I was in Zimbabwe,' said Kioko, as if looking for something to say. 'Then in Zambia.'

'I know.'

Joseph looked up, gaining courage, and stared Kioko in the face.

'Why didn't you write to us?'

Kioko hesitated, and for a moment Joseph saw

some kind of turmoil in his face. Then he frowned, taking refuge behind a show of dignity.

'It was not possible in those places where I was to send a letter.'

He's lying, thought Joseph disgustedly. What about me, and Mama? Ask about us! Go on, ask!

'I was in the copper mines,' said Kioko. 'It was dangerous. My health was not good there.'

Anger was building up inside Joseph now, a creeping, inexorable tide of anger.

Is that all you can say? he thought. After seven years?

'We waited for letters from you,' he said sullenly. 'Mama thought you were dead.'

Say her name now, he thought. Say it now.

'I was planning to return before.' Kioko was looking at a point over Joseph's shoulder, not meeting his eyes. 'It wasn't – I couldn't—'

The weakness in his face snapped the bands holding Joseph's anger in, and it erupted like a volcano spewing out a jet of lava.

'You just left us, Mama and me and Monica! You don't know anything about me. You left us alone! You don't know what it's like when the other boys go with their fathers. You don't care! You just ran away and left us!'

Kioko took a step forward and lifted his right arm.

He's going to hit me, thought Joseph, and for an instant he cowered, as he had done when he was little. Then with a surge of energy he felt his own size and strength.

'No!' he almost screamed. 'You'll never beat me again!'

He leaped backwards and, only half aware of what he was doing, raced towards his camel. He jumped up into the saddle. The camel, seeming to respond to his urgency, lumbered at once to his feet.

'Go!' yelled Joseph. 'Run!'

He flailed at the camel's side with his fists and feet. He was half aware of Boniface and Loipa, who had jumped up and were racing towards him. The camel, nervous and confused, skittered sideways, almost trampling on Tom, who jumped out of its path with a shout. The noise and the sudden movement made the camel panic, and it bolted away, crashing through the bushes.

For a moment or two, Joseph's anger sustained him, then it was swamped by the terror of the ride. The camel was going at a fearful speed, crashing through the trees and bushes. Branches whipped against Joseph's legs and threatened to knock him flying out of the saddle. He could think of nothing but the need to hold on at all costs, not to crash down onto the rock-hard ground so far below.

Then behind him he heard a car's engine starting up. He couldn't look round. He didn't dare for a moment take his eyes off the ground immediately ahead, but he knew his father would be at the wheel. His anger came boiling back again and he stopped feeling afraid.

The camel burst out of the bushes onto an old dry riverbed. The cracked mud had baked to the hardness of tarmac, and the camel put on speed, running as if in a race, jolting Joseph up and down like a sack of flour.

The sound of the car died away. His father had clearly lost his tracks.

Joseph looked over his shoulder. He couldn't see anything except for bare brown earth and dusty trees. He couldn't hear anything except for the flap, flap of the camel's soft feet on the ground and the pounding of the blood in his own ears.

He turned back again, just too late, to see that the camel was veering sideways to avoid a water-hole that some animal had dug in the sand. For a fatal second, he lost his balance, but at the last moment pulled himself back into the saddle. The camel faltered too, seeming to stumble. It righted itself and stood still at last, trembling.

'It's OK. It's OK,' said Joseph awkwardly, trying to reassure it.

He was securely back in the saddle again, but he was trembling too, shaking from head to foot in the aftermath of his fear and anger.

What do I do now? he thought. Where do I go now?

He wanted to dismount. He was trying to

remember what Boniface had said to make the camel kneel, when he felt a judder run through the animal, and it reared its head and let out a terrified scream. It took off again, running faster than ever.

Now Joseph heard a new sound that sent a cold shaft of fear straight to his heart. From the bushes at the edge of the dry riverbed came a deep-throated grunt, and then a tawny streak sprang from its cover.

As if from far away, Joseph heard his own voice screaming, 'Help me! Help!'

The camel was racing for its life, but the lioness was going faster, covering the ground in easy bounds. She was alongside now, looking for a chance to leap up to the camel's throat.

'Go away!' Joseph heard himself yelling stupidly. 'Go away!'

The camel twisted suddenly to the right and Joseph felt a sickening lurch as he was momentarily thrown off the saddle. He saw in a flash the lioness's huge claws, and her red mouth turned up towards him, then miraculously he landed back on the saddle again, and righted himself with a desperate thrust of his hips.

The camel seemed to sense that it couldn't outrun the lioness. It was wheeling round to turn its back on her, trying to land kicks on her belly with its powerful back legs. Joseph, tossed about like a rodeo rider, clung on desperately. His whole world had been reduced to one simple aim, to stay in the saddle, to hold on, only to hold on.

He couldn't see the lioness any more. He didn't dare turn round in case he lost his balance. Then a jolt told him that the camel's kick had hit its mark, and for a moment he felt a surge of relief. But the kick had merely enraged the lioness. Her snarl came again, almost in Joseph's ear. The camel staggered, and Joseph, daring at last to look round, saw that the lioness had leapt onto it from behind. She had locked her claws under its back legs in a cruel embrace, trying to drag it down. Her teeth were fastened on the camel's rump, her head inches from Joseph's back!

The camel was in a frenzy, bucking its legs and twisting its head round as if it wanted to bite at the lioness itself.

No rider could have held on to its tormented back. Joseph felt himself falling, and with a desperate lunge tried to throw himself clear. Then he landed with a thud on the ground.

10

ACCIDENT IN THE SAND

Almost before he had hit the ground, Joseph was scrambling to his feet. The camel was bucking violently, and Joseph could see that the lioness was losing her grip on its rump.

He stood as if paralysed. He was measuring the distance to the trees with his eyes. He wanted to sprint into their cover, leaving the camel to its fate, but he was afraid that if he ran away he would attract the lioness's attention, and she might abandon the camel, which was putting up a terrific fight, and come after him instead.

With a violent kick, the camel dislodged the lioness, who landed heavily on the ground. Her claws had scored triple scarlet stripes down each of the camel's flanks, and there was a jagged wound on its rump where the hide had been torn away by her teeth, but it was still full of fight, bellowing in pain and anger, twisting round and round, still trying to land its kicks.

The lioness, running round in circles to avoid the flailing feet, was now watching Joseph with wide yellow eyes.

She's coming for me! She's going to come after me, he thought frantically.

She was assessing him, choosing her approach. She was crouching now, her tail lashing from side to side, preparing to spring.

Joseph froze. He was holding the lioness's eyes with his, waiting for her to leap so that he could dive away.

She was ready. He could see her bunching her muscles for the spring.

'No!' he screamed. 'Stop it! No!'

Her front legs had already left the ground and the rest of her body was uncoiling after it, when a shot ripped through the air. Joseph had already made his dive, hurling himself to one side, expecting the weight of the lioness to land on him and her claws to slash into him, but the lioness twisted in mid-air. She landed heavily, and Joseph had no more than a glimpse of her, of a confused tangle of golden limbs, before she streaked away, seemingly unhurt, out of the dry riverbed towards the shelter of the bushes.

Joseph looked up and saw the two other camels racing towards him. The ranger was riding the one in front. He was bouncing uncontrollably in the saddle, the rifle still raised to his shoulder. Loipa rode the other camel.

Joseph sank to his knees. He felt a strong urge to be sick and lowered his head, which felt strange, as if he was going to faint.

By the time Loipa and the ranger had dismounted, the feeling had started to wear off and he looked up at them. The ranger was examining the wounded camel, running his hand soothingly over its neck, trying to calm it. Loipa squatted down beside Joseph.

'What happened? Why did you run away?'

Joseph looked up at him, afraid of anger, but Loipa's slim face was only puzzled and concerned.

'I – I'm sorry,' said Joseph weakly. 'It was just – I mean, he . . . '

He broke off. The Toyota had emerged from the bushes higher up the riverbed and was roaring down towards them. It pulled up in a flurry of dust. Kioko was the first to jump out. He raced up to Joseph and Loipa, then stopped abruptly and stood a few feet away looking down at Joseph.

Tom and Afra were hard on his heels.

'Joseph! What happened? Did you fall off your camel? What made you bolt off like that?'

Curiosity and a kind of admiration were alive in Tom's face. Afra dug him in the ribs and gave him a quick meaningful frown.

'Never mind about that. Did you hear the lion? Was he around here? We heard a scary kind of snarling sound and—'

The wounded camel, standing trembling nearby, made a grunting cry as the ranger's exploring fingers probed too close to his wounds.

Afra looked up and saw the unmistakable even rips of the claw marks on its flank. Her mouth fell open.

'It didn't go for you, did it? Oh wow! It did! The lion attacked the camel! Did it get you anywhere? Are you OK?'

Joseph nodded his head gingerly.

'Yes. It was a lioness, not a lion. She jumped on the camel's back. Got her claws behind his back legs. The camel was so brave. He just kicked and bit and shook her off.' He laughed shakily. 'He shook me off, too.'

He tried to stand but his head was still swimming, and he sank down again. He looked up and met his father's eyes. He was waiting for Kioko's anger to break over his head. He was bracing himself for violent words and even blows. But Kioko squatted down beside him and put a tentative hand on his knee.

'You are all right?' he said, speaking in Kikamba, the language of Joseph's childhood. 'You are not hurt?'

A half memory came back to Joseph, an image he'd buried under thick layers of resentment. He'd heard that voice before, the deep hoarseness softened with tenderness. He'd been playing with a ball, out on the road, and a runaway cow had raced past, sending him flying. His father had rushed to pick him up, had held him tightly for a moment or two, and had examined his arms and legs for sore places.

Joseph felt tears sting his eyelids.

'I'm not hurt,' he said gruffly. 'Just a bit sick.'

Kioko stood up.

'I have some water in the car. Wait. I will get it for you.'

He hurried back to the Toyota, opening the driver's door.

Joseph watched him go. He had an awful desire to cry, to burst into noisy sobs, and he tensed his throat and screwed up his eyes to hold the tears back. Then he heard gasps from Afra and Tom and was aware that Loipa, still squatting beside him, was leaping to his feet.

He looked up. In his haste, Kioko had parked the Toyota land cruiser precariously, with the front off-side wheel balancing on a stone. It was already tilting dangerously to one side. He saw, as if in slow motion, his father open the driver's door and put a foot up onto the floor of the car, ready to swing himself inside. Then, as inevitably as a scale going down under a weight, he watched the Toyota tip further over, almost casually at first, then with gathering speed.

Kioko had suddenly become aware of the danger he was in. He jumped out backwards from the driver's seat, landing awkwardly. He staggered, but as he tried to right himself, the car fell with a crash, crushing him under its massive weight.

For a second or two, Joseph stared in horror, unable to move, then he raced forwards.

Only Kioko's head was visible. The land cruiser had landed on his back and he was lying with his face down in the sand.

Joseph stared down at him, then he shut his eyes, unable to bear the sight any longer.

He's dead, he thought incredulously.

He couldn't feel anything.

Loipa was kneeling beside Kioko's head. He was digging frantically, gently turning Kioko's face, trying to free his nostrils from the sand.

Why is he doing that? Joseph thought. Doesn't he know he's dead?

He couldn't believe that this was happening. It was as if he was living through a dream.

Suddenly, Kioko sneezed, and Joseph saw his eyes open for a moment, then shut again.

'Eh, eh, brother,' said Loipa, in cheerful Swahili. 'You are alive! We'll get you out. You'll be all right. Don't worry, my brother.'

He jumped to his feet and shouted to the ranger. In response, the ranger fumbled in his pocket, pulled out a radio handset and handed it to Loipa. Loipa clicked it on.

'Mountview. Come in, Mountview Ranch,' he said.

Joseph heard a crackle of static.

'Accident at Ol Tupesi.' Loipa was walking round the Toyota as he spoke, weighing up what to do, while the ranger knelt down in the sand beside Kioko, and murmured encouragingly to him. 'One man injured, trapped under a car,' Loipa went on. 'Require immediate medical assistance.' There was another burst of static, and Loipa looked round, trying to judge their exact position. 'We are about two kilometres from the airstrip,' he said. 'We will carry him there. We have not yet released him from under the vehicle. It may take time.'

He listened for a moment, then handed the radio back to the ranger, who stood up and took it from him.

'Listen, can you hear me?' Loipa had bent down and was talking to Kioko. 'We will get you out, and take you to a hospital. Do not be afraid.' He stood up again, and gave Joseph's elbow a reassuring squeeze. 'John is coming. He will fly him to the hospital. OK. Let's get him out.'

'Won't it hurt him if you try to pull him?' said Tom.

'No, no, we cannot do that. We must lift the car.' Loipa's eyes were searching the riverbed. 'Tom, Afra, go to the bush over there. Look for some big fallen branches.'

Joseph had been standing motionless, as if in a nightmarish trance. Now he found his voice. It came out in a croak.

'The lioness,' he said.

Loipa frowned.

'You are right. I had forgotten the lioness. We must not go into the bush. We'll do it with stones. Help me, Joseph. The biggest stones we can find. We must raise the land cruiser a little to get him out.'

Joseph realized that he could think again. His mind had cleared. It was racing now, thinking through what had to be done.

'But if we put stones under it, they'll just sink down under its weight into the sand,' he said.

'Yes. Yes!' Loipa hesitated. 'Somehow, we must lift it from him.'

His gaze ran over the group, assessing their strength.

'I don't think we're strong enough to lift it ourselves,' said Afra in a small voice. 'I'd be frightened we'd drop it again if we tried to lift it.'

A soft snickering from one of the camels made Joseph look up. In an instant, he saw what had to be done.

'The camels are strong enough,' he said. 'Are there any ropes in the car?'

Tom grasped his idea at once.

'I'll look,' he said, running round to the back.

Joseph reached the rear door first and lifted it open. A coil of rope, which had been lying neatly on the floor, had been tossed by the fall against the window. Gingerly, trying not to put extra weight on the car, he hooked it out.

Loipa had understood too. He had already grabbed the rope from Joseph and was tying it to the roof rack of the land cruiser.

'Is there another?' he called out to Joseph. 'Two is better. One at each end.'

'Wait. I'll look,' said Joseph, peering into the car again.

He came up a moment later with a second, much shorter rope in his hand.

'Good,' grunted Loipa. 'It's enough. Boniface, bring up the camels.'

Joseph had squatted down again beside his father's head.

'Can you hear me?' he said. 'It's me, Joseph. We're going to get you out.'

He waited, on tenterhooks, for a sign that his father had heard.

If he dies it'll be my fault, he thought desperately. It'll all be because of me.

Kioko's eyes fluttered open for a brief moment. His lips moved as if he was trying to say something, but sand dribbled into his mouth and he gave up the effort.

Joseph jumped to his feet again. He had to push all the bad thoughts away. He had to concentrate only on rescuing his father.

Boniface had brought the two unhurt camels up now and was attaching the ropes to their saddles, looping them in a kind of harness round their chests. Afra watched anxiously.

'Won't it hurt them when they start to pull?' she said. 'Won't the ropes bite into them?'

She had pulled a bundle of old rags out of the car and was quickly arranging them under the ropes to soften their cutting edges.

Joseph and Loipa ran up to check that the knots were tight enough. Loipa pushed Afra out of the way.

'Now!' he shouted.

The ranger delivered a hefty blow to one brown rump, and Loipa struck the other. Boniface, by the camels' heads, was urging them forwards. The ropes took the strain.

'It's lifting!' shouted Joseph, who was back at his post by his father's head. 'Don't stop!'

The land cruiser was rising inch by inch, revealing more and more of Kioko's motionless body. For a horrible moment it stopped and swayed, threatening to crash down again. Joseph let out a yell, and putting his hands under the car, heaved until he thought his arms would crack and his eyes would pop out of their sockets. Then he felt the ropes take the strain again, and the car rise and rise until it was upright.

For one awful moment, it seemed as if the camels would do their work too well and pull the land cruiser right over onto its other side, but Boniface, seeing the danger, halted them.

The land cruiser rocked a couple of times and came to a rest, upright.

'Don't untie the ropes yet!' Joseph called out anxiously. 'It's still tilting!'

Loipa ran round to check on Kioko. Very gently, he and Joseph raised the injured man's head.

'Are your bones broken?' Loipa asked urgently.

'My legs, I think,' said Kioko in a faint growl.

'Your back? Can you feel your back?'

'Yes, I can feel every part of me. My back is not hurt. Only my head and my legs. There is too much pain in my legs!'

Loipa looked up. His face was more cheerful.

'I think you have cheated death this time, my brother,' he said.

Joseph felt his chin quiver. He wanted to cry with relief. Instead he said, 'Can you help me to turn him over?'

Loipa shook his head.

'It is better not to move him. We will touch him only when we have to.'

Boniface and the ranger were adjusting the ropes again, retying one to the front bumper of the land cruiser. Tom was jumping up and down excitedly.

'Yes, she's coming, here she comes!' he called out, as the Toyota, its wheels spinning a little in the soft sand, lurched up onto firmer ground.

'The plane from Mountview! Look there!' shouted Afra, pointing up to the sky.

'We'd better get him into the car then,' said Joseph, 'and drive him to the airstrip.'

A peculiar look came over Loipa's face.

'Boniface!' he called out. 'Can you drive a car?'

Boniface shook his head.

Loipa looked enquiringly at the ranger, who also shook his head.

'We have a problem,' said Loipa, turning back to Joseph. 'None of us can drive!'

11

A NIGHTMARE DRIVE

There was silence for a moment while the impli-
cations sank in. Kioko was moaning quietly and
there was a grey tinge to his face now. Joseph
couldn't bear to look at him.

'I drove once,' he said reluctantly, 'with Uncle
Titus. He showed me, a bit.'

Relief broke out on everyone's faces. Loipa
took control again. He spoke in Maa to Boniface
and the ranger. Very gently, they turned Kioko
over and lifted him. Kioko groaned out loud,
once, and then he fainted. His legs were dangling
horribly. Joseph could not look at them.

What will I say to Mama? he kept repeating in
his head. What if he can never walk again?

He tried to suppress his feelings, to think coolly
and rationally, about what he had to do. He ran
to the land cruiser and jumped into the driving
seat, then he looked round, trying to familiarize
himself with all the dials and levers.

Tom and Afra were behind him, clearing the
back seat of the land cruiser, trying to make a
comfortable place for Kioko. Joseph blocked

them out. He was trying out the gearstick and the steering wheel, testing the pedals with his feet.

I can't do this! I don't remember anything! It's all crazy, he was thinking, trying to stop his mind from shutting down completely as panic threatened to engulf it.

The key was still in the ignition. He turned it, and jumped nervously when the engine spluttered into life.

The men had arrived now. They were gently placing Kioko into the back seat.

'It's a good thing he's unconscious,' muttered Loipa. 'The pain would be too terrible for him.'

Joseph looked for a fleeting moment over his shoulder. His father was lying awkwardly along the back seat of the land cruiser.

'He can't go like that,' he said. 'He'll fall off the seat.'

'No, no. I will hold him.'

Loipa was already lifting Kioko's head and shoulders, easing himself onto the back seat under the injured man so that he could lean his head against his shoulder and cradle him in his arms. As Joseph turned away again, a new emotion caught at his throat, and made him suddenly want to cry. Loipa didn't know Kioko at all. He'd met him for the first time only an hour ago, and yet he was holding him with tenderness, trying to make him as comfortable as he could.

I wish it was me doing that, Joseph thought.

Tom was piling into the front seat of the land cruiser beside him and Afra was climbing up after him.

'Boniface and the rangers are taking the camels,' Tom said. 'They're going to ride in front and look for the best way for the car. All you've got to do is follow them.'

The 'all' sent a brief smile flickering over Joseph's face, but it vanished at once. This was it then. He had to get going now.

He pressed the clutch down and tried to move the gearstick. It grated awkwardly, and seemed unwilling to move.

That's not right, Joseph thought. I'm doing it all wrong!

He shut his eyes for a moment, steadying himself, then tried again. He was getting the feel of it now. The gearstick moved reluctantly into place. Joseph released the handbrake and slowly lifted the clutch. The car jerked forward a little way, and then the engine stalled.

'You have to give it more gas,' Afra said bossily.

Joseph ground his teeth silently. He turned the ignition again, lifted his left foot from the clutch pedal and pumped the accelerator with his right. The car shot forward much too fast. Joseph slammed on the brake and brought it to a halt. He heard Loipa gasp, then murmur reassuringly to Kioko.

'I know what you're doing wrong,' said Afra. 'You have to—'

Joseph cast an imploring sideways glance at Tom. Tom nodded understandingly.

'Afra,' he said savagely, 'if you don't shut up, totally, I mean completely, absolutely, I'm going to kick you out of this car and – and jump up and down on you until you scream for mercy.'

'Hey,' said Afra indignantly. 'I only said—'

She saw that Joseph's eyes were shut and that he was leaning forward, clutching the steering wheel in tense hands.

'OK,' she said, subsiding. 'I get it. Sorry, Joseph. You're doing a great job. Not another word.'

The engine was running smoothly now. Joseph, looking up, saw Boniface and the ranger, mounted on the two uninjured camels, waiting patiently for him further down the dry riverbed. The wounded camel's leading rein was attached to Boniface's saddle.

Joseph took a deep breath and tried again. The sight of the long straight stretch of sand had steadied him. It was no worse than the rough road up north, where, way out in the bush, Uncle Titus had let him take the wheel of his car, and had instructed him in a calm quiet voice, on every move he had to make. He tried to hear that reassuring voice again.

'Good,' Titus would be saying. 'Go on. A bit

faster now. Hear the engine roaring? Change gear. Up to second. Now to third. Keep it steady. Mind that pothole. You're doing fine. That's good. That's really good.'

His confidence was growing. He *was* doing fine. The land cruiser was going at a steady pace, eating up the dry riverbed. The camels had to run now to stay ahead of him.

'Watch out!' Tom gasped suddenly. 'Mind that rock!'

Joseph had seen the rock too. It seemed to have risen suddenly out of the ground. He realized he was going too fast and braked sharply. The land cruiser veered round in a skid. Joseph wrenched the wheel around but the land cruiser didn't respond. For a terrifying moment, he knew he had lost control. Then the car slithered to a halt.

From the back came a groan. Kioko was coming round. Joseph heard him mutter something incoherently, and Loipa murmur a soothing reply. Then Kioko's head seemed to clear as he realized where he was.

'Joseph?' he said, in a slurred voice. 'You are driving?'

'Yes,' said Joseph shortly, starting off again.

There was silence for a moment, then he heard a bark of throaty laughter that ended in a grunt of pain.

'Good boy,' his father said in Kikamba. 'Try

not to brake too hard. This car is a strange one. It stalls all the time.' His voice was growing fainter.

Joseph felt a new thrill of confidence, and a warm feeling settled round his heart. His father had praised him! And even better, he was talking to him as if he was an equal. A friend!

He settled himself back in the driving seat and narrowed his eyes against the brilliant light, looking for the camels. They had halted again, at the edge of the riverbed, and Boniface was pointing sideways into the bush. Joseph's lips tightened. The going would be harder once he'd left the riverbed. He'd have to navigate round trees, and look out for holes in the ground.

A moment later he reached the camels. Boniface leaned down to speak to him.

'The first bit is difficult. We have to go up this bank. Can you do it?'

Joseph's heart skipped a beat. Boniface was pointing up a horribly steep bank, and he couldn't see what was beyond it. He licked his lips.

'I don't think—' he began.

There was an exclamation from the back of the car.

'He's fainted again,' said Loipa. 'He is looking quite bad. We must go on, Joseph.'

Joseph looked desperately down at the gearsticks. There were two, one ordinary one, and another for the four wheel drive, for the really difficult places. He'd often seen Titus use the second gear lever, but he had no idea how to do it.

Tom seemed to read his thoughts.

'You could go back a bit and sort of take a run at it,' he said in a low voice.

Joseph looked behind him. The ground sloped gently away from his back wheels. If he started to slip back down there, he might get stuck in the softer sand near the middle of the riverbed. On the other hand, he didn't have any choice. He looked helplessly for a moment at the ordinary gear lever. The 'R' embossed on it must mean 'Reverse' but he'd never driven in reverse, and he was sure he couldn't do it. He'd just have to let the car roll backwards and hope for the best.

His palms were so clammy they were threatening to slip on the steering wheel. He looked up for a moment and saw Boniface holding the radio transmitter up to his face.

He's telling them to hold on, he thought. Maybe they won't wait for us much longer. Maybe they'll just give up and fly off.

The thought gave him the courage he needed. The car was angled well now. He assessed the steep bank ahead, shut his eyes for an agonizing moment, then lifted the clutch and thrust his foot down on the accelerator. For a second the car stood still, the engine roaring, the back wheels spinning in the soft sand. Then, with a violent jerk, it shot off and up the bank.

Joseph was dimly aware of Tom's gasp and Afra's quickly suppressed whimper. The car had felt at first like the bolting camel, wild and out of control, but now, almost at the top of the bank, it was losing speed. The power seemed to be dying out of it.

His foot was rammed down so hard on the accelerator he was afraid it would go through the floor. His fingers were clenched so tightly round the wheel that the blood had flowed out of them. He was urging the car forward as if it was an animal.

'Go on! Go on!' he was saying in his head, not realizing that the words were pouring out of his mouth. 'You can do it. Keep going! Up, go up!'

The car seemed to hear him. As if it was using its last spurt of energy, it breasted the top of the bank. Joseph slipped it into neutral gear and pulled up. He needed a moment to recover, to stop himself trembling, to wipe the sweat out of his eyes.

Tom and Afra had broken into cries of triumph.

'Wow! You did it! I thought we'd never make it. You're such a genius, Joseph. There was a moment back there, I really thought . . . '

He wasn't listening to them. His eyes had met Loipa's in the mirror. Loipa was frowning and nodding. The unconscious man's head lolled against his shoulder.

'Go on,' he said quietly.

Boniface and the rangers were already moving off. Joseph followed them. He threaded his way around the clumps of trees and bushes, ignoring the scraping, scratching sound of the branches against the sides of the car. His eyes were on the ground, searching out the smoothest way, where there would be the fewest jolts to jar his father.

They came out of the bush suddenly onto a long strip of flat clear land. At the far end of it stood a little white plane.

Joseph began to tear down the straight. There were no obstacles now. He could go fast. He glanced into the mirror again.

We're nearly there, he wanted to say. They'll help you. They'll know what to do.

But this time, he said it in his head.

The camels were racing alongside him, like out-riders to a presidential car. Joseph reached the plane first. John Grant and Sipul had off-loaded a stretcher from the plane and were squatting in the shade of the wing. They stood up and ran out towards him.

'Where's the patient?' said John cheerfully, looking in through the back window of the land cruiser. 'Passed out? Good. It'll be easier to move him.'

His startlingly blue eyes took in Joseph at the wheel, and a quick smile creased the skin on his leathery cheeks.

'You drove this thing? How old are you?'

Joseph couldn't reply. He had turned round and was staring at his father.

'Will he be all right?' he said, knowing his voice was trembling but unable to prevent it.

Sipul and Loipa were already easing Kioko onto the stretcher.

'I should think so.' John was opening the door of the plane. 'There are only leg injuries, aren't there? Nothing wrong with his head or back?'

'No,' said Joseph. John's voice was so reassuring that the word came out as a sigh of relief. 'I don't think so.'

John looked at Joseph more closely.

'Do you know him?'

'Yes,' said Joseph. 'He's my father.'

12

AIR RESCUE

Joseph stood on the rough airstrip, watching the little white plane grow smaller and smaller in the sky.

'Where are you taking him?' he'd asked John.

'To Nairobi. To the main hospital there. They'll have him right in no time.' He'd seen the misery in Joseph's face and had given his shoulder a little shake. 'Look, I'll be back at Mountview this afternoon. I'll send through a bulletin by radio. But don't worry. You'll be back yourselves tomorrow. Prof's coming over to fetch you.'

The last glimpse Joseph had of his father was of the side of Kioko's head, leaning against the headrest of his seat, with Sipul strapped in beside him. He couldn't tell if Kioko's eyes were open or not.

The plane was already no bigger than a distant speck of floating thistledown. A moment later it had disappeared. The others were walking back towards the camels and the land cruiser, but Joseph didn't move. He had a sudden odd feeling that the man in the plane, the man who had come that morning in the land cruiser and who had been crushed when it had toppled over, wasn't his father at all.

He realized that Afra had come back and was standing beside him.

'Can you still see the plane?' She looked up too, screwing up her eyes.

He shook his head.

'No. It's gone.'

Reluctantly, he turned away, and began to walk back with her.

'Is he like you remembered him?' she asked curiously.

'No. That's what I was just thinking.' He was glad she'd asked. 'He was so different. Smaller and, oh, you know, not fierce. I used to be frightened of him when I was a kid. But not now.'

'Yeah. I know what you mean. He used to scare the hell out of me too. But I hardly recognized him. So weird, the way he went bald like that.'

Joseph walked a little faster. He'd forgotten that Afra had known his father too. The thought irritated him. He didn't want to see him through her eyes. He wanted to keep his own mind clear.

They reached the others.

'Are you all right, Joseph?' Loipa said in a low voice, speaking in Swahili. 'You have had a shock this morning. Too many shocks.'

'I'm OK.'

Joseph didn't know how he felt, but he didn't want anyone to ask. He needed time to think.

'What now?' said Tom.

He looked expectant, as if, after a morning packed with action, he was ready for an afternoon of adventures too.

'We have to take the injured camel back to the lodge,' said Loipa, 'and you, too. That is our first priority.'

'But what about the zebra?' objected Afra. 'We were supposed to be looking out for him until we got kind of distracted.'

'The zebra, we will search for him later,' said Loipa. 'It is the middle of the day now. The animals are resting. The lioness will not hunt again until evening.'

Joseph wasn't listening.

I ought to be with him. I should have asked to go with him on the plane, he was thinking.

'But she was hunting just now,' Tom was saying. 'She must have been pretty desperate to go for a camel with a rider on top. Shouldn't we—'

'It is better for you to go back.' Loipa was beginning to look harassed. 'Our first responsibility is to you, our guests. The risk—'

'Oh!' Afra's frown cleared. 'You're worried about our safety! That's all right. We're not scared, one little bit. And we can't just go back and leave the zebra to his fate.' She paused, looking doubtful. 'But then, I guess, the injured camel needs help and . . . '

Joseph's feelings had shifted again.

Why did he come and disturb us? Why did Reverend Samuel have to write that letter? I don't want any of this! I want it to be like it was before.

'I tell you what,' Tom was saying. 'Some of us can take the camels back and some of us can go and see if the zebra's still resting under his tree. Then . . . '

'It doesn't matter what we do!' Joseph burst out suddenly, startling everyone.

'What do you mean?' said Afra. 'The zebra, and the camels—'

'I mean nothing we do will make a difference. If the lioness wants to eat the zebra, we can't stop her. She'll do it sooner or later. If the camel gets better or not, we can't help it.'

'Joseph, have you gone crazy?' said Afra.

'Yes,' said Joseph, and he sat down suddenly on a stone.

There was a stunned silence. Then Joseph shook his head as if to clear away the confused thoughts that had crowded into it. He looked up, saw the concern on everyone's face and laughed shakily.

'I'm sorry,' he said. 'It's OK. I don't mind what we do. I just don't want to drive that car again.'

'You could teach me,' Tom said hopefully. 'I'd love to have a go.'

Afra rolled her eyes.

'Listen, you guys, we've cheated death enough

times for one day. If you want to get behind that wheel Tom, just give me plenty of warning so I can get ten miles away from here first.'

Tom's eyes were half closed. His hands were on an imaginary steering wheel. He was turning it to and fro, making 'thrum thrum' noises.

'Over to the right – yes! We've got her now! Afra Tovey's broken out of cover. She's running down the straight! Ace driver Wilkinson's closing in on her. Yes! He's captured her!'

Joseph stood up and grinned at them. Their normality was making him feel better.

'Oh man,' he said to Tom. 'You can drive that thing all you like. And you can ride a mad camel too. I'm walking from now on.'

Loipa and Boniface had made the two uninjured camels kneel and were calling them over.

'Are you sure? You really want to walk?' said Tom.

'Oh yes,' said Joseph fervently. 'Yes, I really do.'

It was odd walking through the bush with the camels again. It was almost, thought Joseph, as if nothing had happened, as if the arrival of his father and the bolting camel, the accident and the mad drive through the bush had been just a vivid dream. He wasn't even scared of meeting the lioness again. It was as if he'd only imagined her in the first place.

Loipa and Boniface were in a hurry now. They

were urging the camels on. The ranger walked ahead. He held his gun in front of him, and was looking left and right, keenly surveying the bushes on either side.

He stopped and looked round, then spoke in Maa to Loipa.

'The zebra, he was here. He is not far away,' translated Loipa.

'But aren't we miles away from the tree where we left him?' said Tom.

'Not so far,' said Peter. 'We have come round in a circle.'

'Can we find the tree again?' said Joseph. 'We can check if he's still there.'

He wanted urgently, all of a sudden, to know if the zebra was all right. The lioness's open mouth, the sensation of her teeth and claws so near to him, the smell of her hot breath inches away from his back, returned to him in a sickening rush.

'We have to save him!' he said.

The ranger put up a hand to silence him, and Boniface urged the camels quietly to a halt. Everyone held their breath while the ranger stalked on, on silent feet, through the bush. They saw his head emerge above the scrubby little trees as he climbed up a little knoll of rocks. He beckoned cautiously.

Boniface made the camels kneel so that Tom and Afra could dismount, but Joseph, who wasn't riding, was ahead of them. Cautiously, he climbed the rocks and sank down quietly beside the ranger.

He saw at once that this was the same outcrop they'd climbed only this morning, though they'd approached it from a different side. Incredibly, the zebra had hardly moved. He still stood under the tree, but he was more visible now that the sun, moving overhead, had reduced his area of shade. His rump stood out clearly, and one back leg was crooked inwards, only the tip of its hoof resting on the ground. His tail swished gently at the flies on his sides. Joseph could see his wound clearly now. It was healing. There was no doubt of that.

He let out a long sigh. The zebra looked strong, his muscles hard and taut under his spectacular hide. But there was something lonely about him too. A kind of noble sadness.

Joseph thought of the lioness, stalking him through the long grass, then springing out, the cruel weapons of her claws outstretched. She seemed intensely real again. He shuddered, and a cold sweat broke out on his face.

Loipa and the others had arrived now.

'We can't leave the zebra here alone,' he whispered urgently. 'We have to guard him.'

Loipa nodded.

'The ranger will stay here. He has the gun. He will scare the lioness if she comes. But we must return to the lodge now. Come, Joseph. It is time to go back and rest.'

Joseph suddenly knew he was exhausted. He crept down off the rock after Loipa.

'Yes,' he said. 'Yes, let's go and rest.'

13

DELAYED SHOCK

Back in the great room at the lodge, Joseph sank down onto a chair. His limbs felt weak and his knees were actually trembling. He covered them with his hands, afraid that Tom and Afra, who were slumped into chairs nearby, would notice them.

'Are you OK, Joseph?' said Tom.

'Yes,' said Joseph automatically, then he saw that Tom's freckled face was wrinkled with concern. 'No. I don't know. While we were out there, I didn't think so much about the lioness. She didn't seem real to me. But it's strange, now we are here, in safety, I can just see her again, like she was, up on the camel's back, right beside me.'

'What?' Tom's mouth fell open. 'The lioness jumped right up at you? We didn't see that bit. Wow! I'd have been so scared I'd have – I'd have—'

'It was very quick,' said Joseph. 'Then it was over, and then everything else happened, and now I feel really, really strange.'

He didn't want to talk about everything else,

his father's arrival and the accident. He didn't want to think about how Kioko had looked, unconscious, his head lolling against Loipa's shoulder.

'Delayed shock,' said Afra, nodding. 'You have to rest up for a bit. You're supposed to have something sweet. Stay there, and I'll be right back.'

She straightened her long slim legs, which had been tucked under her on the low easy chair, jumped up and went out towards the kitchen. For once, Joseph didn't mind her mothering him. It felt good.

She came back a moment later with a Coke and some sweet biscuits. This time, Joseph didn't bother to hide the shaking of his hands.

'You know what, Joseph,' she said, looking down at him dispassionately. 'Anyone else would either have passed right out, after what you've been through this morning, or they'd be in a fit of screaming hysterics. You're so strong, it's amazing.'

'Yeah. You're something else,' said Tom loyally.

Joseph felt tears fill his eyes. He fought them back, and bit tentatively into a biscuit. Crumbs dropped down onto his T-shirt. He brushed them off awkwardly, not feeling hungry.

'I don't feel very strong,' he said. It was relief to admit it, after all. 'I just feel – I don't know—' He was afraid he would start crying properly, and took a noisy gulp of his Coke.

One of the warriors who had been by the fire the night before came into the room from the direction of the kitchen, almost staggering under a huge tray.

'Loipa says you are very hungry,' he said. His eyes rested on Joseph. 'You especially. You have fought with a lion this morning! And rescued your father! Eh, man, you are the brave one!'

The atmosphere of admiration was taking effect and Joseph was beginning to feel better. He sat up and looked at the tray. There were hard-boiled eggs and a pile of sandwiches, a big potato salad and some thick wedges of cake. Afra was unscrewing the lid of the thermos and peering in.

'Tea,' she said. 'Want some?'

Joseph discovered that he was a little hungry after all. He began to put food on his plate.

'Where's Loipa?' said Tom indistinctly, through a mouthful of sandwich.

'He was in the kitchen a moment ago,' said Afra. 'He says he has things to do this afternoon. He thought we ought to just rest up, and swim and stuff, and he'll see us later. He says he's going to radio Mountview this evening, to see if there's any news of—' she looked awkwardly at Joseph 'of your father.'

The rest of the afternoon passed slowly. They lay about for a while after lunch, too full to move, then drifted up to the beautiful curved pool, which, even in the drought, was fed from a spring inside the hill. It sparkled in the brilliant sun, offering instant coolness and refreshment. They changed quickly and jumped into the water, and their shrieks rang out, down into the ravine below, and up the steep wooded hillside above.

Joseph, floating on his back while Tom practised swimming underwater and Afra sat on the edge of the pool making gentle waves with her legs, thought of the zebra, still standing under his tree perhaps, or, now that the sun was lower, grazing somewhere on the dry grass. Was he safe, or was the lioness prowling nearby? Had he heard the noise the three of them were making? Had it scared him, or had he known it was just young humans having fun, like he and Tom and Afra could tell when young monkeys in the trees in Nairobi were playing a rowdy game?

We think we know so much about animals, he thought, but they know plenty about us, too.

He tried to pursue the thought, mentally counting all the animals who might be within earshot. Anything was better than worrying about his father, wondering whether he was safe in the hospital in Nairobi by now, and what the doctors were saying.

The very thought that Kioko might be injured for life, that he might die even, knotted a tightness in his chest.

Warthog, elephant, waterbuck, he thought

intensely. Zebra, monkey, lion, hyena. Impala, kudu, cheetah.

None of them heard the sound of the Land Rover pulling up below the lodge, so when Prof's long lean figure appeared through the bushes that edged the pool, they all cried out in surprise.

'Prof!' squealed Afra. 'Come on in and swim. It's so good here.'

'Maybe later, honey.'

His eyes were on Joseph.

Loipa's told him everything already, Joseph thought. He wants to know how I am.

He felt reserved. He didn't want to talk about things to Prof. He didn't even know how he felt himself.

'I hear you met with a hungry lioness,' said Prof. He seemed to have read Joseph's reticence, and to have understood. Joseph relaxed a little. He didn't mind talking about the lioness.

'It was, well, it was very terrifying,' he said.

'I'll bet.'

Prof waited a moment, but when Joseph said nothing more, turned to the others. Afra and Tom were already scrambling out of the pool, glancing sideways at Joseph as they related to Prof the events of the morning. Joseph shivered. The sun was going down fast now and it was already a little too cool in the water. He hauled himself out of the pool and walked across the sun-warmed paving to find his towel.

'You didn't come to take us away, did you, Prof?' Afra was saying. 'It's so brilliant here.'

'Not just yet,' answered Prof. 'We can't go now, anyway. It's too late. Tomorrow, maybe.'

Joseph was drying himself. It had occurred to him all of a sudden that Prof might have news of his father, that a radio message might have come through to Mountview from John's plane.

Why doesn't he tell me? he thought. What's happened?

A cold feeling was gripping his insides. Questions were crowding into his mind, but he couldn't ask them. He was glad when Afra said, in a low voice, 'They didn't get a message at Mountview before you left, did they? About Joseph's father?'

Prof shook his head.

'There wasn't time. I came as soon as I heard what had happened. Sounded as if things were getting a little too exciting round here.'

He turned to see Joseph's eyes on him.

'Look, Joseph,' he said, with a reassuring smile. 'From everything Loipa told me I guess things aren't too bad. His head and back weren't hurt, that's the main thing.'

Joseph nodded, and turned away.

Supper was a subdued meal. The food, a succulent joint of roast beef with creamy roast potatoes, and a delicious fruit salad to follow, was eaten in near silence. Darkness had fallen after the brief African twilight, and from the ravine below new sounds rose to the listeners in the lodge – the croaking of frogs in the pool, the harsh loud cries of the tree hyraxes and the distant whoop of a hyena. Another race of animals, the creatures of the night, was stirring now. Mongooses would be hunting, and civet cats. Bushbabies, their saucer-like eyes wide open, would be leaping through the trees, and leopards would be on the prowl.

Tom and Afra were yawning, clearly thinking of their beds. Prof and Sipul were sitting up at the table, involved in a long discussion about the old traditions of Masaailand. Loipa and a pair of other warriors were standing nearby, talking urgently in Maa.

Joseph heard one of them say '*ol-oitiko*', the word for the Grevy zebra, and '*olgnetuny*', which, he knew, meant lion. Nothing else they said made sense. He yawned too. Perhaps, if he went to bed with the others, he'd be able to sleep after all.

A bleeping noise sounded through the great room and Sipul clapped his hand to the radio strapped to the belt that held his red cloth in place.

It's from Mountview, thought Joseph, sitting bolt upright, all thought of sleep banished from his mind. John Grant has returned and he's answering Loipa's call. There's news of Father.

But Sipul was talking in Maa, or rather, he was

listening. He spoke briefly, then hooked the radio back onto his belt.

'Bad news?' said Prof, with a sideways glance at Joseph.

'No, no,' Sipul smiled reassuringly. 'It is the rangers only. The zebra, he is restless. He is moving about as if he can smell the lioness. The rangers have not seen her, but they are sure she is nearby. It is better for some of us to go and help. We will spend the night there, with our brothers.'

He saw Prof's eyebrows rise in a quizzical look.

'It is all right,' he went on hastily. 'We will leave two rangers here at the lodge to guard you in your rooms, in case of incursion by some predators.'

Joseph saw the warriors stand up and begin to move slowly away towards the steps.

I want to go too, he thought, surprising himself. I want to be one of them tonight.

Tom and Afra had stood up and were stretching and yawning.

'I couldn't stay awake another minute,' said Tom, 'not even if you offered me £1,000.'

'Me neither,' yawned Afra. 'Though I feel bad about the zebra. I guess we ought to help guard him too.' She yawned and Joseph held his breath. Then she set off in Tom's wake. 'Are you coming, Joseph?' she said, over her shoulder.

Joseph followed them up the narrow path to

their sleeping room. None of them was in the mood to talk. Tom and Afra were too full of food and too tired out by the events of the day. Joseph was too intent on the plan that was beginning to hatch in his mind.

A few minutes later, all three were under their mosquito nets.

''Night,' said Tom sleepily. 'Hope you sleep well, Joseph. No bad dreams.'

'Thanks,' whispered Joseph.

Afra said nothing. A moment later, regular breathing from both their beds told Joseph they were asleep.

He put a foot cautiously out from under his mosquito net. Neither of the others stirred. He wriggled free of the clinging white muslin. He hadn't changed into his pyjamas. All he had to do was put on his shoes.

He'd been afraid that the warriors would be far away already, that they'd have loped off into the night down some path known only to them, and that he'd never be able to catch them up.

He needn't have worried. As he tiptoed out of the sleeping room, pausing at the ends of Tom's and Afra's beds in case a creaking floorboard gave him away, he could hear the murmur of young men's voices ahead of him on the path running down to the parking place.

Then, from the great room above, he heard Prof's voice call out, 'Good night, Sipul, thanks for everything,' and Prof's feet scrunching on the path.

He'll be going into the sleeping room next to ours, thought Joseph. He'll be passing this way.

He shrank back into the cover of the bushes beside the path. Prof's tall unsuspecting form strode quickly past him and turned into the second sleeping room. Cautiously, hoping that Prof would think any footsteps he heard were Sipul's, Joseph crept out of his hiding place, went up the path and into the big room. No one was there. He ran across it, to the head of the steps leading down to the parking place.

Below, he heard sounds again. Footsteps. Low voices. A burst of quiet laughter. There was a half-moon tonight, only just risen, but by its weak light he could see well enough.

The dim shapes of a line of warriors moved below him. Quickly, he began to bound down the steps after them.

14

THE LIONESS MEETS HER MATCH

Joseph tried to move silently as he followed the line of men. He wanted to be well away from the lodge before they discovered his presence. The last thing he wanted was to be sent back to bed in disgrace. But he had reckoned without Loipa's sensitive ears, trained to pick up the slightest sound in the surrounding bush.

As he stole forwards down the path, he realized too late that the shapes he was following had disappeared. He went on a few steps, then gasped with fright as strong hands came out of nowhere and gripped his arms.

There was a grunt of surprise and he was released almost at once.

'Joseph!' said Loipa, stepping out of the shadow of a tree. 'What are you doing? We thought you were a poacher. You were lucky we did not use our spears on you at once.'

Joseph tried to read the expression on his face. The moonlight glinted on Loipa's high cheekbones, but the hollows of his eyes were shadowed.

'I wanted to come with you,' he said lamely. 'I don't know. I – just came.'

He couldn't see the frown on Loipa's face but he could hear the disapproval in his voice.

'This is not good,' he growled. 'You are our guest at Ol Tupesi. We are responsible for your safety.'

'I know, but I don't want to be a guest,' Joseph cried. 'I want to be a warrior!'

He was aware that he sounded childish, but he couldn't help it.

Some of the warriors broke into quiet laughter, but one or two were muttering to each other. Joseph could see that there were eight or nine of them. All of them carried a spear.

'If you were a Maasai boy,' Loipa said at last, 'I would send you home to be disciplined by your father, but you are a Kamba, and our guest, and our brother. It is all right. You can come with us. We will teach you things tonight.'

He turned his head, and Joseph could see that he wasn't frowning now.

The others were already setting off again.

'Go in front of me,' Loipa said in a low voice. 'Move quickly and silently. Do not step on a stick or a stone. Use your eyes and ears well.'

Joseph began to walk. The *shuka* of the man in front, which was dulled to a sombre grey in the moonlight, made a block of shadow. It was disappearing fast. The warriors were moving with silent skill, avoiding bushes, placing their sandalled feet deftly on the ground. Their heads turned constantly, their eyes scanning the bushes on either side, their ears tuned to pick up the slightest sound.

There was a rhythm to their walk, a spare economy of movement. They were going fast, and Joseph had to struggle to keep up with them. He was aware all the time of Loipa behind him, at the end of the line. Once, Loipa's spear appeared alongside him, holding back the branches of a bush that threatened to brush noisily against Joseph's side. A little later, he grabbed Joseph's shoulder and almost wrenched him off the path. Looking down, Joseph saw the rope-like body of a long snake uncoiling by the path. He didn't have time to react with the horror that would normally have filled him. He stepped around it and went on.

His mind was empty of everything except for the dangers of the night. Once or twice he thought, Where are we going? When are we going to stop? but a moment later his sharpened ears would pick up the distant sound of galloping hooves, or the rattle of a porcupine's quills, or an unidentifiable rustle in the undergrowth nearby that sent shivers down his spine.

At last the warriors halted. They stood on a patch of bare ground and in low voices discussed their position. Joseph couldn't follow their rapid Maa, but he watched their tall lean figures, the outline of their hard frames softened by the *shukas* they were wearing, their naked arms and legs gleaming dully in the white light of the moon which glinted on the deadly metal points of their spears. He watched their gestures, their raised hands and pointing chins, trying to follow their meanings.

'Is the zebra near here?' he whispered to Loipa. 'Do you know where to look for him?'

'Yes, we know. The rangers told us on the radio to come to this place, but they have not waited for us. They have gone further after him, I think.'

One of the warriors had crouched down and was examining the ground. He beckoned to the others.

'The zebra's prints,' said Loipa. 'He has found them.'

Joseph peered over the warrior's shoulder. He could see nothing on the ground except for a few meaningless marks in the sand. He looked at the warrior again. The young man was casting about in the dust, looking for more signs.

'There, he has found the rangers' tracks,' said Loipa with satisfaction. 'The zebra went fast away from here and the rangers were running after him. Now we must follow.'

The march went on again. It was slower now. The warriors were following faint tracks in the dust. They had to stop every few metres to pick up the trail again. Joseph found it hard to slacken his pace. He'd got used to their silent speed. It had excited him and he wanted to go fast again. But patience, he could see, was part of the warriors' training. They waited without fuss while the expert among them studied the ground, and Joseph, marvelling at his ability to see even in the dim moonlight, followed him confidently when he'd shown them the way.

Joseph settled into the new pattern, copying the warriors' every move, and the sound, when he heard it, gave him a shock, making him start with fear. No more than a hundred metres ahead came a violent growl, a familiar terrible rasping snarl. The lioness was hunting again.

Instinct made Joseph want to turn and run blindly away into the bush, but a stronger impulse was urging him to stay close to his companions. He was wondering which way they would run when he saw, to his horror, that they were moving as fast as they could towards the terrifying noise, right into the circle of danger.

He could feel the hairs rise on his head. He had only one desire now, to stay as close to Loipa as he could. Resisting the temptation to clutch at Loipa's *shuka*, he raced along beside him.

The warriors ahead had stopped suddenly, and Loipa and Joseph almost ran into them. They had come out of the thick scrub to a more open area. Dry grass, grey in the moonlight, rippled in the breeze. The warriors were standing in the dense shade of a tree, invisible to anything beyond it, watching, like an audience on the edge of a circus ring, a terrible battle being fought before their eyes.

The lioness had found the zebra. She had clearly been chasing him for he had stopped running. He was standing, his flanks heaving, his great head tossing, uncertain from which direction she would charge at him again.

Joseph could see the lioness now and a shiver ran through him, puckering his skin. She was down in the grass, almost invisible. Her silken body, lowered as far as it would go, was brushing along the ground as she inched forward on silent paws.

As Joseph watched, she broke suddenly from cover, and like a streak of molten silver, tore across the ground towards the restless zebra. Beside him, Joseph heard the warriors draw in their breath and raise their spears.

They can't, he thought in disbelief. They can't take on a lioness with nothing but their spears.

But Loipa put up an authoritative hand. The spears dropped. Joseph looked up at him.

'She'll kill him,' he whispered.

'Wait,' murmured Loipa.

The lioness was almost on the zebra now. She was leaping for his neck, trying to pull him down so that she could suffocate him with the mighty clamp of her jaws on his throat. But the zebra, his stripes a blur of black and white, turned at the last second, and while she was still in mid-air, he lashed out with his tremendous hooves. The kick caught the side of her head and she dropped like a stone.

Joseph wanted to give a whoop of triumph, and run out and do a victory dance over the fallen lioness, but Loipa put a restraining hand on his arm, and looking round, Joseph could see that none of the other warriors had moved an inch. They stood like statues under the cover of the trees.

The zebra hadn't waited to savour his triumph. With a defiant toss of his magnificent head and a flicker of his round ears, he took off, trotting away across the grass. A few minutes later, he was invisible in the dim distance.

The warriors let out their collective breath and emerged into the moonlight. They approached the lioness cautiously. She lay still, and Joseph could see, even from this distance, that the life had gone out of her. The warriors reached the lioness, and one prodded her gently with the butt of his spear. She didn't move.

Joseph came up, and looking down at her he felt an odd stirring of pity. The side of her head had been crushed by the zebra's mighty kick. She must have died at once. She looked smaller now, almost forlorn, the fearsomeness of her teeth and claws diminished, her snarls silenced forever.

'Perhaps she had cubs waiting for her,' Joseph

said, regret in his voice. 'Perhaps that's why she was so desperate for a kill.'

Loipa bent down to examine her dugs.

'No, there is no milk here,' he said. 'She is old. Look, her fur is thin here, and here.'

He touched the lioness's back. Joseph, trying to repress a lingering shudder of irrational fear, followed his example. The lioness's fur was surprisingly rough and wiry.

'Why didn't you drive her off yourselves?' he asked Loipa. 'I thought you were going to run out at her with your spears.'

'It is better for the zebra to do his own work,' Loipa said, walking away from the lioness. 'She was a little old and tired. I could see that. But the zebra looks big and strong. I thought she will not be able to take him. If he can repel his enemies himself, he will be safer. He will become more bold and confident. Also, we cannot watch him forever. He must find his own way.'

'He didn't even know we were there,' said Joseph.

'That's good. It was a spear that made his wound. It was thrown by a man. He will always fear men now, and if he sees us he will run far away and Ol Tupesi will lose him.'

The other warriors were calling out greetings to the two rangers, who had suddenly emerged at a swift trot from the bush. The rangers were scratching their heads and laughing with embarrassment as the warriors teased them.

'They lost the zebra,' Loipa told Joseph, 'then they lost themselves.'

The rangers had seen the lioness. They went up to examine her, and one of them raised the dead creature's head, admiring her ferocious teeth.

'She is old now, but she was a powerful one once,' Loipa said admiringly. 'Our zebra, he is noble and strong to kill her. Come, Joseph, the hyenas will soon be here. The lioness is prey for them. Let us leave them to their feast.'

'Are we going back then, to the lodge?' asked Joseph, unable to keep the disappointment out of his voice.

'To the lodge? No.' Loipa had started off already, but he looked over his shoulder and grinned at Joseph. 'Now we will make our fire and talk and sing, and be warriors until sleep overtakes us. Come. Follow me.'

15

A NIGHT WITH THE WARRIORS

It was different now, walking with the warriors. They were still alert, still using every sense in case of unseen danger, but they were no longer hunting, or afraid of being hunted. They talked, and their pace was slower.

They had been climbing for a while, and came out onto a promontory. It was above the stream, and even in the dim light Joseph could see that it commanded a sweeping view across the countryside.

'This is our place,' Loipa said, helping the others to collect sticks for the fire.

The warriors were relaxed now. They were laughing and teasing each other. Every now and then one of them threw a cheerful remark in Swahili to Joseph.

'So, Kamba boy, how do you like our Maasailand?'

'Come on, sit here by us. You have seen a victory over a lioness. This night you will never forget!'

The fire was soon blazing brightly. The young men squatted round it, leaning on their spears, their voices rising and falling in the musical rhythms of their language, laughing with each other, at ease in the deep familiarity of old companionship.

Joseph looked round at them enviously. The firelight lit up their bronze faces and cast long shadows behind them so that, already tall, they looked even more magnificent. Their bright beaded necklaces and bracelets shone as they moved.

'Loipa,' one of them called out. 'Have you adopted this boy? Have you made him your son?'

Joseph turned happily from one friendly face to the other. He liked their teasing. It made him feel like one of them. He shifted his feet. He wasn't used to squatting for such a long time, and he was afraid that his calves would begin to cramp up, but he didn't want to show his discomfort.

Loipa sighed.

'My son!' he said, leaning forward to poke at the fire with a stick. 'When my son is grown like Joseph, I hope he will be so brave.'

'Have you really got a son?' said Joseph, surprised. 'I didn't think you were married.'

'I am a senior warrior,' Loipa said. 'We are permitted to marry. I have had my wife for two years. My son is a year old.'

Joseph digested this in silence. He had thought of Loipa as a friend, an older brother almost, of the same generation. It was strange to think he was a father. It made him seem further away.

'What's he like, your baby?'

Loipa beamed with pride.

'He is very fine. A very fine boy. He will go to school and be a great man.'

'Taller than his father!' one of the warriors called out.

Loipa stretched his back to look as tall as possible.

'He will respect me, that is the most important thing. He will learn respect for his elders.'

'Is it the most important thing?' asked Joseph doubtfully, remembering his childhood fear of the glowering face of his father. 'But you don't want him to be afraid of you, do you?'

'Afraid? No!' Joseph heard a momentary hesitation in Loipa's voice. 'Respect for the elders of the Maasai, and for the warrior traditions, for us that's the first thing. But he will learn the modern way also, to go to school and university.'

'How can he do both?' asked Joseph, puzzled. 'How can he be a warrior and a student too?'

Loipa stirred the fire again.

'He'll find a way.'

'It's so different in Nairobi,' Joseph burst out. 'We don't have so many of the old traditions. Everyone lives separately. Afra and Tom are my friends, but their lives are – it's just different. I can't explain it. They don't worry too much about respect for their parents. They speak to them in such familiar ways.' He stopped. 'Afra and Prof, they're more like brother and sister. Like friends. It's very confusing.'

'Things are changing,' said Loipa. The other warriors were quiet now. They were listening too. 'Our fathers used to go all the time together with the other young men into the bush, and they lived with their cattle and hunted with their spears. My father, he was alone once with his cows, and he killed a big lioness who was chasing his calf. He's a great man, but he never learned to read.'

'I don't know anything about my father,' said Joseph unhappily. 'He went away to look for work when I was little.'

Loipa grunted, unsurprised.

'A man has to do that. He has to go and find work. It doesn't matter. If you didn't know him then, soon you'll be a man and you'll discuss everything with him. He'll choose a wife for you.'

Joseph let out a crack of laughter.

'A wife! No, I wouldn't let my father choose my wife! I'm going to choose my own, but not for years and years.'

The other warriors laughed.

'Choose your wife?' said one.

'Listen to him!' said another. 'He wants to be in love!'

Joseph felt a distance opening up between them. He didn't know what to say. The subject hung uneasily in the air. Then one of the warriors began to sing, in a high, melancholy voice. Loipa, watching Joseph's face, translated the words for him.

> 'Oh black beautiful lady,
> Oh black beautiful lady,
> You are the one I will follow.
> Do you admire me?
> Do you like my fine necklace of beads?
> If you go, and I know you will go,
> If you go, and I know you will go,
> Back to your village to marry another,
> Remember me!
> Remember me!'

Joseph felt a kind of longing, a new feeling. It made the blood rush to his face. The song ended, and someone coughed. Another warrior put more wood on the fire, sending a shower of sparks up into the dark air.

'When I get married, I won't ever leave my wife and children,' said Joseph, a little louder than he had intended.

Loipa sighed.

'Look at me,' he said. 'To work here, at Ol Tupesi, I must leave my wife and son in the village. I see them when I can.'

'My mother had a good job, in a *mzungu*

house,' said Joseph passionately. 'My father didn't need to go away.'

Loipa's nose wrinkled.

'A man doesn't like to live on his wife's money. He will feel too bad.'

Joseph thought about this. His grandfather had told him once that his father was a proud man. Maybe it was his pride that had made him go away.

'Well anyway, I won't ever beat my children,' cried Joseph. 'Never!'

Loipa smiled.

'You're right. It's best to talk to them, not to beat them. But it's so hard to be a parent. All the time you worry, how to look after them, how to bring them up to be good men. Our fathers did things in one way, and always they disciplined us severely, but there are new ideas now. My father, he would never be permitted to sit with his own father, my grandfather, but I'll always let my son sit with me. We're looking for new ways, half in our old traditions, half with the modern ideas.'

The fire was dying down now and the warriors were beginning to yawn. One by one they wrapped themselves in their *shukas* and lay down on the ground. Joseph lay back too. The air was a little cold, but the glowing embers of the fire warmed him. He looked up at the sky.

The moon was setting. Soon it would disappear over the edge of the horizon and only the stars would be left, but they blazed so brilliantly against the blackness that they even cast a faint radiance on the earth.

His eyes were wide open as he watched them, trying to trace their slow movement across the vault of infinite blackness. He felt as if he'd been two people for a long time, living in two worlds. His life in Nairobi, the life he shared with his mother, and his school, and Tom and Afra, was only part of him. The other part, deeply buried inside him, came from the village where Grandfather lived. He had found it here, too, with the warriors. And this other, deeper part, which he hadn't thought about so clearly until now, was the bit of him that might be able to understand his father.

What had Kioko said? 'Good boy. Try not to brake too hard. This car is a strange one.'

It wasn't much to go on, but it was a start. Perhaps Loipa was right, and his father had only been trying, all those years ago, to teach him respect, only he'd gone about it in the wrong way. Perhaps now they'd be able to start talking to each other. A picture of Kioko lying under the land cruiser came into his mind and he shivered, pushing it away. He didn't want to think about the accident, and his father's injuries. He'd worry about that when he had more news.

He'll get better, he told himself. He's got to. He'd better not try to get me a wife, that's all.

The idea of a wife was so ridiculous it made him smile, and the smile turned into a yawn. The stars above seemed too brilliant now, and watching them was making his head spin. He closed his eyes.

A cough woke him. He stirred, feeling the unaccustomed hardness of the bare ground beneath him before he had even opened his eyes. It was cold too. He shivered and reached down to pull his *shuka* up round his shoulders, only to find that no blanket was there.

He remembered where he was and opened his eyes.

The sky was still dark, but greyness, tinged with pink, was spreading from the east. All around the long-dead fire the warriors were stirring, rising to their feet and rearranging their *shukas*, clearing their throats and greeting each other in voices still thick with sleep.

Joseph propped himself up on one elbow.

'Are we far from the lodge?' he asked Loipa, who was stirring the grey ashes to make sure that every last ember had been extinguished.

'No, not far.' Loipa pointed with his chin along the ridge. 'We'll go back now. Your friends will wake soon. They'll be worried about you.'

Joseph stood up and hugged his chilled arms to his chest. The sky was lightening minute by minute, and as he watched, the dazzling rim of the sun shot up over the horizon, bathing the whole world in a golden glow. Heat was in even its first sparse rays and Joseph stretched, welcoming it gratefully.

Then he heard one of the warriors gasp and point down to the plain below.

'*Ol-oitikoishi*,' he said. 'Look there!'

A herd of animals, some big, some small, was picking its way delicately towards the stream. Their diamond patterned heads nodded up and down as they walked and their crisp manes riffled in the morning breeze.

'Five, six, seven, eight – there are eight of them!' breathed Joseph. 'Eight Grevy zebra!'

Beside him Loipa was sucking in his breath with pure delight.

'Five mares,' he crowed softly, 'and three foals. It is the beginning of a real herd! They heard our stallion calling and they've come to him. This is a wonderful thing for Ol Tupesi!' He turned and gripped Joseph's shoulder, kneading it almost painfully in his excitement. 'Look at them! They're exploring. They're asking themselves, Do we want to stay in this place? Yes, look! They're drinking now. They like our water. They'll stay here with us, I'm sure they'll stay!'

In the distance came a familiar sound. The Grevy stallion had begun his morning round, walking the boundary of his territory, calling out his challenge and his invitation as he went. The mares lifted their heads from the water and, as the crystal drops fell from their muzzles, they twisted their ears to listen to the sound.

'They like his song,' one of the warriors said gleefully. 'They want him for their husband.'

He gave a whoop of triumph and the others echoed it, then together, laughing and slapping each other joyfully on the back, they set off at a trot along the path to the lodge.

Joseph, following close behind them, was urging them in his head to go faster.

There'll be news of him by now, back at the lodge, there's got to be, he thought. The confidence he'd felt in the night evaporated, and his stomach curdled with anxiety.

16

RAIN!

Joseph peeped into the sleeping room. Two shapeless lumps, obscured by mosquito netting, were lying motionless. Afra and Tom were still asleep. He felt relieved. He didn't want to talk about the night's experiences. They belonged to his other world, his other life. He crept past them and went out through the other side of the room where a few rough hewn steps on the hillside led down to a shower.

When he came back, clean and refreshed, the others were getting up.

'Where did you go in the night?' asked Tom. 'I woke up and you weren't there.'

His face was so open and friendly that Joseph decided to tell him everything after all.

Tom and Afra are my friends, he thought. If they don't understand this they won't know me at all.

'I followed Loipa and the warriors,' he said. 'We spent all night out in the bush.'

'Wow! That's amazing!' Tom looked impressed.

Afra, standing up from putting on her shoes, pursed her mouth in a silent whistle.

'We talked a lot. About, oh, getting married, and bringing up your children and – and fathers and everything.'

Tom had looked incredulous at the beginning of this speech but he was nodding understandingly by the end.

'Loipa, he's like me, a bit,' Joseph went on. 'I mean, he understands about the old traditions, and respect, and discipline. When we danced with the warriors yesterday, I just wanted to be one of them, and I thought I was, a bit. But last night I found out that they're not like me at all in other ways. Do you know they let their fathers choose their wives for them?'

Afra shook her head.

'No. Oh no! Let Prof choose a husband for me? Some archaeological gargoyle with bits of old pottery in his pockets and his head stuffed full of dates? No way, baby.'

Joseph grinned.

'That's what I thought.' He saw they were still looking at him and went on, struggling to find the right words. 'But I liked being with them. Nairobi and everything there, and you – especially you – are part of me, the biggest part really. But I'm sort of like the warriors too. It's the part that knows Grandfather and the village, I think.'

'Yeah. I know what you mean.' Tom looked at him respectfully. 'I know there's different bits of you, that is. It makes you kind of special, like I'm sometimes not sure which of you I'm talking to. It's good, though.'

'It's your deep African soul,' said Afra lightly, though her eyes were serious. 'If you want to know, I'm jealous of it, in a way. I've never got too close to my Ethiopian soul, and now I'm afraid it's buried too deep and I won't ever be able to dig it out. Anyway, welcome home, Joseph. You've been away for a while, you know that?'

Joseph reached for the baseball cap that was slung on a chair near his bed and put it on with the brim askew.

'Yes. I've been in another place. It was good there, but it's nice to be back, too.'

Footsteps sounded on the gravel path outside and Prof appeared.

'You guys slept well?'

He didn't notice their swift exchange of glances.

'Like logs,' said Afra casually.

'Good. I thought you'd like to know, Joseph, we've had a call from Mountview. John says to tell you that it's looking good for your father, better than he'd thought. He's broken his right femur, quite badly, and his left ankle's a bit crushed, but they'll be able to get him as good as new again. He was dopey yesterday because he'd concussed himself – hit the side of his head on the ground when he fell. He'll come out of that soon enough, with time and plenty of rest. Oh, and you needn't worry about the car, either. The garage in Nanyuki is sending someone out for it.'

Joseph's face had been expanding into a great grin of relief, but it clouded over again as a new worry occurred to him.

'Will he have to stay in hospital a long time, and have some operations on his legs? It will cost a lot of money. Mama—'

Prof nodded.

'It was the first thing on his mind when he came to his senses. I'd radioed John, to tell the hospital I'd help out with the bill, but your father, boy, he's a proud one! "I don't need help from anyone," he said. "My savings will be sufficient." '

Joseph felt a stirring of pride himself. He nodded, pleased.

'When are we going back?' he asked, suddenly longing to leave.

'After breakfast.' Prof looked at his watch. 'We have to go by Mountview to pick up my stuff. There's a long day's driving ahead.'

'I'll be sorry to go,' Afra said. 'This is just the best place. I'm going to worry about the zebra stallion, and whether the lioness gets him.'

'Oh, I didn't tell you!' Joseph broke in. 'The lioness is dead! She tried to get the zebra, but he fought back and he kicked her so hard on the head, like this—' he jumped up and shot one leg out backwards, narrowly missing his bedpost. 'It

157

was so amazing. The lioness just fell down dead. She was all silver in the moonlight. And then—'

He stopped, aware of Prof's puzzled eyes on him. He felt the blood rush to his face.

'I – I went out last night with the warriors. It was just me. Tom and Afra didn't even know.'

Prof's brows snapped together.

'You went rambling round the countryside in the middle of the night without telling anyone?'

'Loipa was there.' Joseph was watching him anxiously. 'And there were many warriors with us. Loipa didn't want me to come. I asked him, and then he let me. And it was wonderful, Prof. Really, really wonderful. I thought the lioness would get him, the zebra I mean, but she was old, Loipa said, and the zebra, he was so strong. And the best thing was this morning, because when we woke up we saw them, a whole herd of Grevy mares and foals. They've come to Ol Tupesi.'

'Oh! That's incredible!' cried Afra. 'Where are they? Can we see them?'

Prof was still frowning.

'You stayed out all night?'

Joseph shifted his feet, but kept his eyes on Prof's face, without letting them fall.

'Yes. Loipa and the warriors, they're my brothers.'

Prof looked at him for a moment longer, then a smile twitched at the corner of his mouth.

'I see. Well, let's go and find out what your brothers have rustled up for breakfast, OK?'

It was later than Prof had intended when they finally left Ol Tupesi. He had been caught up in a long conversation with Sipul, who was telling him about some interesting caves he and his brother had found when they were children further along the escarpment.

'Did you see anything unusual lying around in there?' Prof kept asking him. 'Bits of pottery? Bones, maybe?'

'It was a long time ago,' Sipul answered patiently. 'I was a child. Really, I cannot remember.'

Joseph, Tom and Afra left them to it and went to the edge of the great room, scanning the countryside below with eager eyes, hoping to see the zebras.

Loipa joined them. He looked up at the sky and held up a hand to test the breeze.

'If the rains come at all, it will be very soon. If they don't—'

He didn't finish, but Joseph saw that his eyes were on the stream in the ravine below which, even since yesterday, seemed to have shrunk to an even narrower ribbon.

It was time to leave at last. Joseph, torn between a wish to stay and a longing to go, overheard Loipa ask Prof for a lift to Mountview Ranch.

'I have to discuss our new zebras with John,' he said. 'It is best for them if they can pass easily backwards and forwards between Mountview and Ol Tupesi, like the elephants do. We must see what can be done to help them.'

Joseph was glad he was coming with them. It was a wrench leaving Ol Tupesi behind, but at least they'd have Loipa for a few hours longer.

They peered into every bush as the Land Rover jolted away from the lodge, hoping for a glimpse of closely patterned black and white stripes. Nothing was there.

'It's the middle of the day now.' Loipa glanced at the shadows on the ground, which had shrunk to almost nothing under the trees. 'They're resting somewhere under a tree.'

It was quite noisy in the Land Rover. Loipa and Prof, in the front seat, were engaged in a long conversation about budgets and financing, while Joseph, sandwiched between Tom and Afra in the back, was telling them in detail, all over again, about the amazing death struggle of the zebra and the lioness.

They had been driving through the north end of Mountview Ranch for a long time, and were almost at the long low thatched office buildings in the middle of the ranch when Joseph broke off abruptly. The bright sunshine, which they had taken for granted for many months now, was suddenly dimmed and through the open window of the Land Rover came a startling chill.

Joseph looked over his shoulder.

'Behind us!' he shouted. 'Look!'

Everyone looked round. A dark wall of indigo cloud was rushing towards them out of the sky. Drifts of rain hung from it, like the tasselled fringe of a curtain. Loipa let out a shrill yell of excitement. The wind that carried it along was bringing a smell that brought an ecstatic expression to his face as he breathed it in.

'Rain!' he cried, pummelling his knees with his balled fists. 'The rains are coming!'

The first huge drops hit, splattering down on the windscreen and making runnels in the dust as they ran off. They came singly at first, then, the next moment, the full deluge hit them.

Loipa, in a frenzy of excitement, was fumbling at the Land Rover door as if he wanted to jump out while it was still going. Just in time, Prof pulled up outside the office. A moment later, Loipa was outside, his arms lifted, while the rain poured off him in streams.

'Thank God! Thank you God!' he shouted.

Joseph hesitated for a moment, then he scrambled over Tom and dived out of the car too, and Tom and Afra followed. They were soaked in a moment, as if they'd stood under a shower, but the rain was so intense, so wild and exciting that they couldn't stop themselves from staggering around in it, shrieking with laughter, holding their arms up to let the water run down inside their dripping sleeves. They were already soaked to the skin, but it felt as if they were getting gloriously wetter all the time.

The whole of nature seemed to be dancing too. Wreaths of steam rose from the baked earth, which had turned from a dull grey to a deep terracotta. A delicious smell, like fresh baked bread, rose from it. The brittle grey stems of dead grass and the withered leaves on the bushes were now a rich ochre colour, and birds, in a frenzy of excitement, were fluttering from branch to branch, shaking showers of silver droplets off their quivering feathers. Joseph and the others shrank back in sudden alarm when a group of elephants, too close for comfort, came running past, the water cascading down their backs, turning their dusty brown hides to a gleaming dark grey. They were gone a moment later, and the intensity of the storm seemed to go with them.

Joseph, pausing for breath, saw that the distant mountains, which had been invisible a moment ago, were emerging again, a faint blur of purple, as if an artist had daubed them in with washes from his watercolour box.

A moment later, the rain stopped, the last few drops hurrying as if to catch up with the others, and pale patches of blue appeared in the sky.

'Wonderful! It's wonderful!' cried Loipa, his dripping *shuka* hanging limply from his shoulder. He wiped water from his cheeks. 'Now we can be happy. The good times will come.'

17

COMING HOME

They reached Nairobi later than Prof had meant to. It was scary being out on the roads after dark. They dropped Tom at his house first, and as Prof turned the Land Rover in through the gateway into the compound of the Tovey's dilapidated bungalow, Joseph saw the light shine out from the porch and the figure of Sarah, his mother, standing there, her arms folded, a forbidding frown on her face. His heart sank.

'Flakjackets at the ready, everyone,' Afra said softly. 'Sarah's finger's on the trigger.'

Sarah waited until they were out of the Land Rover. They stood in front of her like a row of naughty schoolchildren. She ignored Prof and Afra and turned to Joseph.

'What have you all been doing? That is what I want to know!'

'Mama,' began Joseph. 'It's all right, really it is.'

Her chest was heaving.

'It's all right? What is all right! I get a telephone call this morning from some strange person up there in Maasai country. The line is so bad I cannot hear him hardly at all. He says my husband was searching for his son, he has had a serious accident, he is in hospital in Nairobi, his legs are crushed. He doesn't tell me which hospital he is talking about, so I cannot discover what this news means. I have been waiting all day, all *day . . .* '

She burst into tears.

Prof had been bending down to greet a wriggly little dog who was leaping up, delirious with pleasure at seeing him again. Now he stood straight again.

'Sarah, I'm so sorry.'

'Why did you not call me?' Sarah sniffed mightily and searched in the pocket of her roomy dress for a handkerchief.

'But I didn't know they'd call you from up there,' said Prof reasonably. He tried to hold off the puppy from pawing at his trousers. 'Get down, Wusha! Honestly, Sarah, I had no idea. I was going to tell you all about it when we got home.'

While he was still speaking, Joseph put an arm round his mother's broad waist and led her into the kitchen.

'I found him, Mama.' He was speaking in Kikamba now. 'He was in the garage, like the Reverend said. At least, he wasn't there himself, but it was the place where he works.' They sat down at the kitchen table. Outside they could hear Prof and Afra unloading the bags from the Land Rover. 'The next day he came to where we were staying to find me.'

'But the accident? He had an accident?'

'It was my fault.' Joseph picked up a teaspoon lying on the table and worked it round unnoticingly between his fingers. 'When he found us, I felt just so angry. So *furious*, I didn't want to speak to him. He looked at me without a smile, as if he wanted to beat me. I – there were camels there. I jumped onto one and it ran away with me.'

Pure astonishment flooded Sarah's face.

'Camels? You rode a *camel*?'

'Yes, Mama, but that wasn't the worst bit. There was a lion in the bush there and it attacked my camel and I fell off.' He stopped and swallowed. 'I thought it was going to kill me!'

Sarah, speechless, was staring at him in disbelief.

'And then the rangers came and fired, and the lion ran away, and Father came up in the car. It was a land cruiser and it was such a strange car, Mama. You mustn't brake too hard because it stalls all the time.'

Sarah waved the car away with one dismissive hand.

'But the accident? What happened?'

'I'm telling you! Father stopped and got out, then he went back to the car to – to get some water for me, and it, the car I mean, was balanced on a stone, and it tipped over on top of him.' Joseph shuddered. He could see the scene again in front of his eyes as if it had only just happened. 'It was so horrible. I didn't know what to do.'

He dropped the teaspoon with a clatter and wiped his eyes vigorously on his sleeve.

Sarah leaned forward and put one soft arm round his neck. He pulled away from her.

'We got him out and I drove the car to the airstrip. I drove it, Mama.'

He paused, waiting for a reaction, but Sarah hadn't seemed to notice this, the most extra-ordinary part of his story.

'There was a doctor there? They examined him? How badly is he hurt?'

Joseph was startled by the intensity in her voice. She really cares about him, he thought. He was astonished. All his life he'd only noticed her anger for his father. For the first time he understood her love. Something fell into place in his head.

'It looked bad at first,' he said, his voice more confident now, 'because he wasn't quite con-scious.' He saw again the frightening grey tinge in Kioko's face and the way his head had lolled on Loipa's shoulder. He wouldn't tell her about that. 'His legs looked bad, too. There wasn't a doctor there, but we heard later that he had hit his head and he had concussion, and one leg is broken and the other ankle is crushed a little bit, but the doctors at the hospital can put it right. He will be quite OK again.'

Sarah jumped to her feet and marched across to the cupboard above the fridge where, ever since Joseph could remember, she had kept all her papers and money in a black tin box. She took it down and opened it, then pulled out a wad of notes and a bank book.

'There will be enough maybe,' she said, looking through them doubtfully.

'He doesn't want your money,' said Joseph. 'He told them he has enough savings himself.'

She wasn't listening to him.

'I can borrow more if I need to. Reverend Samuel himself told me if I need anything . . .'

Joseph stood up and shook her arm.

'Mama, listen. He's going to pay for the hospital himself. He told them. He has the money.'

'Eh, well, that's something new,' said Sarah, sitting down at the table again. She looked almost disappointed, as if her pride had been dented.

Pride, thought Joseph. That's what there is in my family. Too much pride.

'Tomorrow is Sunday,' Sarah was saying. 'I'll go to visit early. I will see what he has to say for himself. He will require some food, some decent things to eat. I had better put some peas in to soak now.'

She stood up and went over to a cupboard.

Joseph yelped with surprise as something buffeted him unexpectedly from behind. A goat, its curly brown hair glossy with health, was butting him with its sharp little horns.

'My goat!' he said delightedly.

'That goat,' said Sarah, looking at the little creature in disgust. 'Take him away out of the kitchen. Afra? Afra! Have you let out all the animals? You will hear what I have to say if that goose comes in here, on my clean floor!'

She marched out of the kitchen.

Joseph gently fondled his goat's silky ears, letting them slip through his fingers. Outside he could hear Wusha's ecstatic barks, the honks of Stumpy the goose and the soft hoots of Kiksy, Afra's pet bushbaby.

He leaned back in his chair and smiled. It was good to be home again.

Joseph stood at the side of the bed and stared down at his father. Sarah, who had been at Kioko's bedside when he had arrived, had gone away as soon as he had appeared.

Joseph wished she'd stayed. Kioko looked small and somehow shrivelled, lying on the iron bedstead, his eyes closed.

What am I going to say when he wakes up? thought Joseph. What's he going to say to me?

He studied his father's face. The flesh had shrunk a little and Joseph could see the broadness of his forehead, even more obvious now that his hair had thinned, and the sharpness of his lower jaw.

It's like mine, thought Joseph, fingering his own chin.

He'd prepared himself for this moment, planning out what he'd say if his father was angry with him, but now that he was here, and Kioko was lying helpless and asleep in front of him, all the speeches he'd made up in his mind had evaporated out of his head.

Kioko stirred, and as if he felt Joseph's eyes on him, opened his own. His whole face broke into a smile of delight. He struggled as if he wanted to sit up, and managed to lever himself a little way up his pillows. By the time he was settled comfortably again, Joseph could see that he was struggling to quench his smile and regain his dignity. Joseph didn't mind. In that first moment of wakefulness, of undisguised truthfulness, he'd seen what he wanted to see.

He pulled up a chair that was standing by the wall nearby and sat down. Then he folded his hands and waited.

Kioko said nothing.

'Are you feeling better?' Joseph asked at last in Kikamba. 'Do your legs hurt you?'

Kioko pulled off the thin blanket that covered him and Joseph saw that both legs were encased in plaster.

'They'll be all right, the doctor says. They hurt a little. It's not too bad.'

'I'm sorry,' Joseph began.

He wanted to say more, but the words wouldn't come. Kioko looked embarrassed, as if he didn't know what to say either.

He's like me, Joseph thought, surprised. He doesn't know how to say things.

'It's all right,' said Kioko gruffly. 'It was not good, to leave the car in that place. But I was confused. The camels and the lion, they were taking all my attention. Eh, eh, Joseph, you gave your father a fright.'

His chest heaved with suppressed laughter.

'I know. I'm sorry. I—'

'Who taught you to drive?' interrupted Kioko. 'Don't tell me. Titus. I know.' He frowned, as if the thought of his successful, competent brother-in-law made him feel uncomfortable. 'He's a bad teacher. Never showed you how to use the four wheel drive.'

'He only gave me one lesson.' Joseph dropped his eyes. He resented any criticism of Uncle Titus, who had been much more like his real father than the man on the bed in front of him. And yet, for the first time, he could understand that Kioko might resent Titus too.

'What happened about the car?' he said. 'Did the garage in Nanyuki make a big fuss about it?'

'They fired me.' Kioko grimaced as he shifted

his position. 'I've lost a month's wages. But they can't do anything else to me. It doesn't matter. I was thinking I would move somewhere else, anyway.'

'Move somewhere else? Where? Where did you want to go?' Joseph felt a tightening in his chest, a mixture of hope and dread.

'I wasn't sure.' Kioko glanced up at him, then looked down again. 'After all these years it seemed—' he hesitated 'difficult to come home. I was thinking about Uganda, maybe. There is work there.'

'And now?'

Kioko was looking over his shoulder. Sarah was standing in the doorway of the room. She seemed to have teamed up already with a group of other women who were bringing in plates of hot food for their sick husbands. They were laughing, shaking their heads and rocking from side to side.

Joseph looked back at his father. Kioko's face was doubtful. He hesitated, as if a struggle was going on inside him.

'I will see,' Kioko said. 'I cannot go anywhere until my legs are better, at least.' His face broke into a smile. 'Anyway, someone must teach my son how to drive properly. What does Titus know about cars?' He snapped his fingers. 'Nothing!'

The bus that took Joseph and Sarah home from the hospital was crowded with people. The two of them sat crammed against each other on the back seat. Joseph's mind was buzzing with questions.

'What will happen now, Mama?' he asked, raising his voice above the roar of the noisy old engine.

'I don't know,' she said. She looked out of the window. Joseph followed her gaze. A group of unemployed men were squatting in the shade of a tree. 'Your father has to work. It will be hard for him to find a job here, and he is used to living alone. Perhaps he will go. Perhaps he will stay. He will come and go, maybe, and live with us some of the time.'

'But if he stays, where will we live? Will you still work for Prof? Will we move somewhere else?'

She looked down at him with surprise.

'Of course I will work for the Professor! How can I leave Afra? She is like my own child. Who will take care of her whenever the Professor goes away?'

Joseph thought of Afra greedily gulping down Sarah's cookies, and Afra pouring out to Sarah an account of a bad day at school, and Sarah bending over Afra to take a splinter out of her foot.

Another worry occurred to him.

'But Father always said that our place at Prof's, it wasn't big enough for us all.' He was thinking of the little house that he and Sarah shared in the garden of Prof's bungalow.

'Oh!' Sarah tossed her head. 'For years the Professor has said to me, "Sarah, I will make you a bigger house," and I have always told him no. I have enough work in the bungalow. Do you think I want to look after another big place? But now, I will accept it. It will be good to add another room.'

'But will Father like us to stay there? Will he make us go?'

She sniffed.

'Your father cannot tell me, after all these years, where I should go or what I should do.' Her voice had been sharp, but now it softened. 'But he has told me, he prefers us to have our own house. He has money now and he wants to buy a place himself. Your father – and I – we will buy a house and rent it out. And when we are old it will be there for us.'

Joseph tried to imagine the future, his father staying sometimes, perhaps, then going away again to look for work.

'Even if Father goes away, he will come back, won't he?' he said. 'He won't just disappear again, for years and years?'

He was surprised at himself. A week ago he would never have believed he'd want his father to come home. Now he felt a kind of anticipation, even excitement, at the thought.

'No, no.' Sarah nodded comfortably. 'He promised me. Never again. He also does not want to lose us another time, Joseph. He suffered, I think.' She smiled down at him. 'He loves you. You are his son.'

Joseph didn't meet her eye.

'Did he say that himself? Really?'

She hesitated.

'He tried to. You don't know him so well yet. He cannot say things easily. But he tried. And I know what he means. I know him. I can read what his eyes are saying. He loves you. You must believe me.'

Joseph turned his head to look out of the window. A man was driving a herd of cows down the road, whacking their hides with his stick, and making clouds of dust billow up.

As he watched, the cows' brown sides seemed to melt away, and instead he saw a maze of black and white striped flanks that shimmered as they moved through the long grass. Where were the zebras now? Had the stallion joined the herd of mares? And if he had, would they all stay together?

It was starting to rain again. Fat drops were making discoloured blobs on the dry ground and people were beginning to run for cover.

The stream at Ol Tupesi, he thought. It'll be filling up now.

He closed his eyes. He could see everything

clearly: the lodge halfway up the steep hillside, the warriors in their *shukas* and the pool beneath the trees where the animals came to drink.

The Grevy stallion must have found the mares by now, he thought. They'll be together.

He could imagine them, meeting each other for the first time. The stallion would arch his neck and take a few prancing steps, trying to impress the mares, who, their foals beside them, would step lightly into the territory he had marked out for himself. They'd look around for a while, Joseph supposed, trying to decide if they would stay, or if they would move on somewhere else, to find another mate and another territory. But if they did stay, they'd walk together, and stand, in quiet moments, in the shade of the trees by the stream, and the stallion and the mares would groom each other, while the foals played beside them.

Elizabeth Laird
Wild Things 3:
ELEPHANT THUNDER

'Elephants,' said the wildlife ranger, 'are the most dangerous animals in Africa.'

Tom has never seen an elephant in the wild. He's always loved the massive, majestic beasts – and now Titus Musau is taking him and Joseph to Mount Kenya to observe them at close quarters. Despite the warnings, Tom can't wait to get there.

But nothing could have prepared him for his first elephant encounter. A young, wounded bull, screaming in pain and rage, and charging straight for him!

Elizabeth Laird
Wild Things 4:
RHINO FIRE

It is the rhino's only chance of survival . . .

As the animal charges away from the speeding helicopter,
Titus leans perilously out to take aim with his long dart gun.
If only the rare black rhino can be relocated to a new reserve,
Afra and Joseph know it might join the few others of its
kind.

But as Nakuru the rhino faces a far greater danger. Men
armed with powerful rifles, who will kill for its valuable horn.
And who are ready to shoot any child that tries to stop
them . . .

Elizabeth Laird
Wild Things 5:
RED WOLF

The wolf's coat was a vivid russet colour, luxuriously thick.
His deep amber eyes looked fearlessly into Afra's.

On a desolate mountain plateau, Afra comes face to face
with one of the rarest animals in the world – the Ethiopian
wolf. The survival of this beautiful creature somehow seems
deeply connected with her quest to find out if her long-lost
family is alive. Her desperation to save the wolves makes
her take a terrible risk to protect a den of pups. A risk that
puts Afra herself in serious danger . . .

Elizabeth Laird
Wild Things 7:
PARROT RESCUE

The parrot seemed to be thinking. He flashed his brilliant
flame-coloured tail feathers.
  'Wanna nut,' he said.

Tom and Afra are having a great time looking after an
amazing African Grey parrot. But they know that thousands
of these birds die in the cruel trade that smuggles wild parrots
out of Africa. Then Tom boards a flight from Nairobi to
England and notices a man carrying a suspicous package.
All alone, at London's vast airport terminal, Tom knows he
must act fast – and sets off on a reckless and dangerous
chase . . .

WILD THINGS titles
available from Macmillan

The prices shown below are correct at the time of going to press.
However, Macmillan Publishers reserve the right to show new retail
prices on covers which may differ from those previously advertised.

ELIZABETH LAIRD

1. Leopard Trail	0 330 37148 7	£2.99
2. Baboon Rock	0 330 37149 5	£2.99
3. Elephant Thunder	0 330 37150 9	£2.99
4. Rhino Fire	0 330 37151 7	£2.99
5. Red Wolf	0 330 37152 5	£2.99
6. Zebra Storm	0 330 37153 3	£2.99

All Macmillan titles can be ordered at your local bookshop
or are available by post from:

**Book Service by Post
PO Box 29, Douglas, Isle of Man IM99 1BQ**

Credit cards accepted. For details:
Telephone: 01624 675137
Fax: 01624 670923
E-mail: bookshop@enterprise.net

Free postage and packing in the UK.
Overseas customers: add £1 per book (paperback)
and £3 per book (hardback).